Robert Smythe Hichens

The Folly of Eustace

And other stories

Robert Smythe Hichens

The Folly of Eustace
And other stories

ISBN/EAN: 9783744750790

Printed in Europe, USA, Canada, Australia, Japan

Cover: Foto ©Andreas Hilbeck / pixelio.de

More available books at **www.hansebooks.com**

The Folly of Eustace

And Other Stories

By
Robert S. Hichens
Author of An Imaginative Man, The Green Carnation, Etc.

New York
D. Appleton and Company
1896

CONTENTS.

THE FOLLY OF EUSTACE.

I.

SOME men deliberately don a character in early youth as others don a mask before going to an opera ball. They select it not without some care, being guided in their choice by the opinion they have formed of the world's mind and manner of proceeding. In the privacy of the dressing-room, the candles being lighted and the mirror adjusted at the best angle for a view of self, they assume their character, and peacock to their reflection, meditating: Does it become me? Will it be generally liked? Will it advance me towards my heart's desire? Then they catch up their cloak, twist the mirror back to its usual position, puff out the candles, and steal forth into their career, shutting the door gently behind them. And, perhaps till they are laid out in the grave, the last four walls enclosing them, only the dressing-room could tell their secret. And it has no voice to speak. For, if they are wise, they do not keep a valet.

At the age of sixteen Eustace Lane chose his mask, lit the candles, tried it on, and re-solved to wear it at the great masquerade. He was an Eton boy at the time. One fourth of June he was out in the playing-fields, pay-ing polite attentions to another fellow's sis-ter, when he overheard a fragment of a con-versation that was taking place between his mother and one of the masters. His mother was a kind Englishwoman, who was very short-sighted, and always did her duty. The master was a fool, but as he was tall, hand-some, and extremely good-natured, Eustace Lane and most people considered him to be highly intelligent. Eustace caught the sound of his name pronounced. The fond mother, in the course of discreet conversation, had proceeded from the state of the weather to the state of her boy's soul, taking, with the ease of the mediocre, the one step between the sublime and the ridiculous. She had told the master the state of the weather—which, for once, was sublime; she wanted him, in return, to tell her the state of her boy's soul —which was ridiculous.

Eustace forgot the other fellow's sister, her limpid eyes, her open-worked stockings, her panoply of chiffons and of charms. He had heard his own name. Bang went the door on the rest of the world, shutting out even feminine humanity. Self-consciousness held him listening. His mother said:

"Dear Eustace! What do you think of him, Mr. Bembridge? Is he *really* clever? His father and I consider him unusually intelligent for his age—so advanced in mind. He judges for himself, you know. He always did, even as a baby. I remember when he was quite a tiny mite I could always trust to his perceptions. In my choice of nurses I was invariably guided by him. If he screamed at them I felt that there was something wrong, and dismissed them—of course with a character. If he smiled at them, I knew I could have confidence in their virtue. How strange these things are! What is it in us that screams at evil and smiles at good?"

"Ah! what, indeed?" replied the master, accepting her conclusion as an established and very beautiful fact. "There is more in the human heart than you and I can fathom, Mrs. Lane."

"Yes, indeed! But tell me about Eustace. You have observed him?"

"Carefully. He is a strange boy."

"Strange?"

"Whimsical, I mean. How clever he may be I am unable to say. He is so young, and, of course, undeveloped. But he is an original. Even if he never displays great talents the world will talk about him."

"Why?" asked Mrs. Lane in some alarm.

To be talked about was, she considered, to be the prey of scandalmongers. She did not wish to give her darling to the lions.

"I mean that Eustace has a strain of quaint fun in him—a sort of passion for the burlesque of life. You do not often find this in boys. It is new to my experience. He sees the peculiar side of everything with a curious acuteness. Life presents itself to him in caricature. I—— Well hit! Well hit indeed!"

Someone had scored a four.

The other fellow's sister insisted on moving to a place whence they could see the cricket better, and Eustace had to yield to her. But from that moment he took no more interest in her artless remarks and her artful open-worked stockings. In the combat between self and her she went to the wall. He stood up before the mirror looking steadfastly at his own image.

And, finding it not quite so interestingly curious as the fool of a master had declared

it to be, he lit some more candles, selected a
mask, and put it on.

He chose the mask of a buffoon.

．　　　．　　　．　　　．　　　．　　　．

From that day Eustace strove consistently
to live up to the reputation given to him by
a fool, who had been talking at random to
please an avid mother. Mr. Bembridge knew
that the boy was no good at work, wanted to
say something nice about him, and had once
noticed him playing some absurd but very
ordinary boyish prank. On this supposed
hint of character the master spoke. Mrs.
Lane listened. Eustace acted. A sudden
ambition stirred within him. To be known,
talked about, considered, perhaps even wondered at—was not that a glory? Such a
glory came to the greatly talented—to the
mightily industrious. Men earned it by labour, by intensity, insensibility to fatigue,
the "roughing it" of the mind. He did not
want to rough it. Nor was he greatly talented. But he was just sharp enough to see,
as he believed, a short and perhaps easy way
to a thing that his conceit desired and that
his egoism felt it could love. Being only a
boy, he had never, till this time, deliberately
looked on life as anything. Now he set himself, in his, at first, youthful way, to look on

it as burlesque—to see it in caricature. How
to do that? He studied the cartoons in *Vanity Fair*, the wondrous noses, the astounding
trousers, that delight the cynical world. Were
men indeed like these? Did they assume such
postures, stare with such eyes, revel in such
complexions? These were the celebrities of
the time. They all looked with one accord
preposterous. Eustace jumped to the conclusion that they were what they looked, and,
going a step farther, that they were celebrated
because they were preposterous. Gifted with
a certain amount of imagination, this idea of
the interest, almost the beauty of the preposterous, took a firm hold of his mind. One
day he, too, would be in *Vanity Fair*, displaying terrific boots, amazing thin legs, a fatu-
ous or a frenetic countenance to the great
world of the unknown. He would stand out
from the multitude if only by virtue of an
unusual eyeglass, a particular glove, the fashion of his tie or of his temper. He would
balance on the ball of peculiarity, and toe
his way up the spiral of fame, while the music-hall audience applauded and the man-
agers consulted as to the increase of his sal-
ary. Mr. Bembridge had shown him a weapon
with which he might fight his way quickly to
the front. He picked it up and resolved to

use it. Soon he began to slash out right and left. His blade chanced to encounter the outraged body of an elderly and sardonic master. Eustace was advised that he had better leave Eton. His father came down by train and took him away.

As they journeyed up to town, Mr. Lane lectured and exhorted, and Eustace looked out of the window. Already he felt himself near to being a celebrity. He had astonished Eton. That was a good beginning. Papa might prose, knowing, of course, nothing of the poetry of caricature, of the wild joys and the laurels that crown the whimsical. So while Mr. Lane hunted adjectives, and ran sad-sounding and damnatory substantives to earth, Eustace hugged himself, and secretly chuckled over his pilgrim's progress towards the pages of *Vanity Fair*.

" Eustace! Eustace! Are you listening to me ? "

" Yes, father."

" Then what have you to say ? What explanation have you to offer for your conduct ? You have behaved like a buffoon, sir—d'you hear me ?—like a buffoon ! "

" Yes, father."

" What the deuce do you mean by ' yes,' sir ? "

Eustace considered, while Mr. Lane puffed in the approved paternal fashion What did he mean ? A sudden thought struck him. He became confidential. With an earnest gaze, he said :

" I couldn't help doing what I did. I want to be like the other fellows, but somehow I can't. Something inside of me won't let me just go on as they do. I don't know why it is, but I feel as if I must do original things —things other people never do ; it—it seems in me."

Mr. Lane regarded him suspiciously, but Eustace had clear eyes, and knew, at least, how to look innocent.

" We shall have to knock it out of you," blustered the father.

" I wish you could, father," the boy said. " I know I hate it."

Mr. Lane began to be really puzzled. There was something pathetic in the words, and especially in the way they were spoken. He stared at Eustace meditatively.

" So you hate it, do you ? " he said rather limply at last. " Well, that's a step in the right direction, at any rate. Perhaps things might have been worse."

Eustace did not assent.

" They were bad enough," he said, with a

simulation of shame. "I know I've been a fool."

"Well, well," Mr. Lane said, whirling, as paternal weathercocks will, to another point of the compass, "never mind, my boy. Cheer up! You see your fault—that's the main thing. What's done can't be undone."

"No, thank heaven!" thought the boy, feeling almost great.

How delicious is the irrevocable past— sometimes!

"Be more careful in future. Don't let your boyish desire for follies carry you away."

"I shall," was his son's mental rejoinder.

"And I dare say you'll do good work in the world yet."

The train ran into Paddington Station on this sublime climax of fatherhood, and the further words of wisdom were jerked out of Mr. Lane during their passage to Carlton House Terrace in a four-wheeled cab.

.   .   .   .   .   .

"What an extraordinary person Mr. Eustace Lane is!" said Winifred Ames to her particular friend and happy foil, Jane Fraser. "All London is beginning to talk about him. I suppose he must be clever?"

"Oh, of course, darling, very clever; otherwise, how could he possibly gain so much notice? Just think—why, there are millions of people in London, and I'm sure only about a thousand of them, at most, attract any real attention. I think Mr. Eustace Lane is a genius."

" Do you really, Jenny ?"

" I do indeed."

Winifred mused for a moment. Then she said :

" It must be very interesting to marry a genius, I suppose ?"

" Oh, enthralling, simply. And, then, so few people can do it."

" Yes."

" And it must be grand to do what hardly anybody can do."

" In the way of marrying, Jenny ?"

" In any way," responded Miss Fraser, who was an enthusiast, and habitually sentimental. " What would I give to do even one unique thing, or to marry even one unique person !"

" You couldn't marry two at the same time —in England."

" England limits itself so terribly; but there is a broader time coming. Those who see it, and act upon what they see, are pioneers; Mr. Lane is a pioneer."

"But don't you think him rather extravagant?"

"Oh yes. That is so splendid. I love the extravagance of genius, the barbaric lavishness of moral and intellectual supremacy."

"I wonder whether the supremacy of Eustace Lane is moral, or intellectual, or—neither?" said Winifred. "There are so many different supremacies, aren't there? I suppose a man might be supreme merely as a—as a—well, an absurdity, you know."

Jenny smiled the watery smile of the sentimentalist; a glass of still lemonade washed with limelight might resemble it.

"Eustace Lane likes you, Winnie," she remarked.

"I know; that is why I am wondering about him. One does wonder, you see, about the man one may possibly be going to marry."

There had never been such a man for Jane Fraser, so she said nothing, but succeeded in looking confidential.

Presently Winifred allowed her happy foil to lace her up. She was going to a ball given by the Lanes in Carlton House Terrace.

"Perhaps he will propose to you to-night," whispered Jane in a gush of excitement as the two girls walked down the stairs to the carriage. "If he does, what will you say?"

"I don't know."

"Oh, darling, but surely——"

"Eustace is so odd. I can't make him out."

"That is because he is a genius."

"He is certainly remarkable—in a way. Good-night, dear."

The carriage drove off, and the happy foil joined her maid, who was waiting to conduct her home. On the way they gossipped, and the maid expressed a belief that Mr. Lane was a fine young gentleman, but full of his goings-on.

Jane knew what she meant. Eustace had once kissed her publicly in Jane's presence, which deed the latter considered a stroke of genius, and the act of a true and courageous pioneer.

Eustace was now just twenty-two, and he had already partially succeeded in his ambition. His mask had deceived his world, and Mr. Bembridge's prophecy about him was beginning to be fulfilled. He had done nothing specially intellectual or athletic, was not particularly active either with limbs or brain; but people had begun to notice and to talk about him, to discuss him with a certain interest, even with a certain wonder. The newspapers occasionally mentioned him as a

dandy, a fop, a whimsical, irresponsible creature, yet one whose vagaries were not entirely
without interest. He had performed some
extravagant antic in a cotillon, or worn some
extraordinary coat. He had invented a new
way of walking one season, and during another season, although in perfect health, he
had never left the house, declaring that movement of any kind was ungentlemanly and
ridiculous, and that an imitation of harem
life was the uttermost bliss obtainable in
London. His windows in Carlton House
Terrace had been latticed, and when his
friends came there to see him they found
him lying, supported by cushions, on a
prayer-carpet, eating Eastern sweetmeats
from a silver box.

But he soon began to tire of this deliberate imprisonment, and to reduce buffoonery
to a modern science. His father was a rich
man, and he was an only child. Therefore
he was able to gratify the supposed whims,
which were no whims at all. He could get
up surprise parties, which really bored him,
carry out elaborate practical jokes, give extraordinary entertainments at will. For his
parents acquiesced in his absurdities, were
even rather proud of them, thinking that he
followed his Will-o'-the-wisp of a fancy be-

cause he was not less, but more, than other young men. In fact, they supposed he must be a genius because he was erratic. Many people are of the same opinion, and declare that a goose standing on its head must be a swan. By degrees Eustace Lane's practical jokes became a common topic of conversation in London, and smart circles were in a perpetual state of mild excitement as to what he would do next. It was said that he had put the latchkey of a Duchess down the back of a Commander-in-Chief; that he had once, in a country house, prepared an apple-pie bed for an Heir-apparent, and that he had declared he would journey to Rome next Easter in order to present a collection of penny toys to the Pope. Society loves folly if it is sufficiently blatant. The folly of Eustace was just blatant enough to be more than tolerated—enjoyed. He had by practice acquired a knack of being silly in unexpected ways, and so a great many people honestly considered him one of the cleverest young men in town.

But, you know, it is the proper thing, if you wear a mask, to have a sad face behind it. Eustace sometimes felt sad, and sometimes fatigued. He had worked a little to make his reputation, but it was often hard labour to live up to it. His profession of a buffoon sometimes exhausted him, but he could no longer dare to be like others. The self-conscious live to gratify the changing expectations of their world, and Eustace had educated himself into a self-consciousness that was almost a disease.

And, then, there was his place in the pages of *Vanity Fair* to be won. He put that in front of him as his aim in life, and became daily more and more whimsical.

Nevertheless, he did one prosaic thing. He fell in love with Winifred Ames, and could not help showing it. As the malady increased upon him his reputation began to suffer eclipse, for he relapsed into sentiment, and even allowed his eyes to grow large and lover-like. He ceased to worry people, and so began to bore them—a much more dangerous thing. For a moment he even ran the fearful risk of becoming wholly natural, dropping his mask, and showing himself as he really was, a rather dull, quite normal young man, with the usual notions about the usual things, the usual bias towards the usual vices, the usual disinclination to do the usual duties of life.

He ran a risk, but Winifred saved him, and restored him to his fantasies this even-

ing of the ball in Carlton House Terrace.

It was an ordinary ball, and therefore
Eustace appeared to receive his guests in
fancy dress, wearing a powdered wig and a
George IV. Court costume. This absurdity
was a mechanical attempt to retrieve his
buffoon's reputation, for he was really very
much in love, and very serious in his desire
to be married in quite the ordinary way.
With a rather lack-lustre eye he noticed the
amusement of his friends at his last vagary;
but when Winifred Ames entered the ball-
room a nervous vivacity shook him, as it has
shaken ploughmen under similar conditions,
and for just a moment he felt ill at ease in
the lonely lunacy of his flowered waistcoat
and olive-green knee-breeches. He danced
with her, then took her to a scarlet nook, apparently devised to hold only one person, but
into which they gently squeezed, not without
difficulty.

She gazed at him with her big brown eyes,
that were at the same time honest and fanci-
ful. Then she said:

"You have taken an unfair advantage of
us all to-night, Mr. Lane."

"Have I? How?"

"By retreating into the picturesque

clothes of another age. All the men here must hate you."

"No ; they only laugh at me."

She was silent a moment. Then she said:

"What is it in you that makes you enjoy that which the rest of us are afraid of ?"

"And that is——"

"Being laughed at. Laughter, you know, is the great world's cat-o'-nine-tails. We fear it as little boys fear the birch on a winter's morning at school."

Eustace smiled uneasily.

"Do you laugh at me ?" he asked.

"I have. You surely don't mind."

"No," he said, with an effort. Then: "Are you laughing to-night ?"

"No. You have done an absurd thing, of course, but it happens to be becoming. You look—well, pretty—yes, that's the word —in your wig. Many men are ugly in their own hair. And, after all, what would life be without its absurdities ? Probably you are right to enjoy being laughed at."

Eustace, who had seriously meditated putting off his mask forever that night, began to change his mind. The sentence, " Many men are ugly in their own hair," dwelt with him, and he felt fortified in his powdered wig. What if he took it off, and henceforth Wini-

fred found him ugly? Does not the safety
of many of us lie merely in dressing up? Do
we not buy our fate at the costumier's?

"Just tell me one thing," Winifred went
on. "Are you natural?"

"Natural?" he hesitated.

"Yes; I think you must be. You've got
a whimsical nature."

"I suppose so." He thought of his journey with his father years ago, and added: "I
wish I hadn't."

"Why? There is a charm in the fantastic, although comparatively few people see it.
Life must be a sort of Arabian Nights Enter-
tainment to you."

"Sometimes. To-night it is different. It
seems a sort of Longfellow life."

"What's that?"

"Real and earnest."

And then he proposed to her, with a laugh,
to shoot an arrow at the dead poet and his
own secret psalm.

And Winifred accepted him, partly because she thought him really strange, partly
because he seemed so pretty in his wig, which
she chose to believe his own hair.

They were married, and on the wedding-
day the bridegroom astonished his guests by
making a burlesque speech at the reception.

In anyone else such an exhibition would have
been considered the worst taste, but nobody
was disgusted, and many were delighted.
They had begun to fear that Eustace was
getting humdrum. This harlequinade after
the pantomime at the church—for what is a
modern smart wedding but a second-rate
pantomime?—put them into a good humour,
and made them feel that, after all, they had
got something for their presents. And so
the happy pair passed through a dreary rain
of rice to the mysteries of that Bluebeard's
Chamber, the honeymoon.

II.

WINIFRED anticipated this honeymoon
with calmness, but Eustace was too much in
love to be calm. He was, on the contrary,
in a high state of excitement, and of emotion, and the effort of making his ridiculous
speech had nearly sent him into hysterics.
But he had now fully resolved to continue in
his whimsical course, and to play for ever
the part of a highly erratic genius, driven
hither and thither by the weird impulses of
the moment. That he never had any impulses but such as were common to most
ordinary young men was a sad fact which he
meant to most carefully conceal from Wini-

fred. He had made up his mind that she
believed his mask to be his face. She had,
therefore, married the mask. To divorce her
violently from it might be fatal to their happiness. If he showed the countenance God
had given him, she might cry: "I don't know
you. You are a stranger. You are like all
the other men I didn't choose to marry."
His blood ran cold at the thought. No, he
must keep it up. She loved his fantasies because she believed them natural to him. She
must never suspect that they were not natural. So, as they travelled, he planned the
campaign of married life, as doubtless others,
strange in their new bondage, have planned.
He gazed at Winifred, and thought, "What
is her notion of the ideal husband, I wonder?" She gazed at him, and mused on his
affection and his whimsicality, and what the
two would lead to in connection with her
fate. And the old, scarlet-faced guard smiled
fatuously at them both through the window
on which glared a prominent "Engaged" as
he had smiled on many another pair of fools
—so he silently dubbed them. Then they
entered Bluebeard's Chamber and closed the
door behind them.

Brighton was their destination. They
meant to lose themselves in a marine crowd.

They stayed there for a fortnight, and then returned to town, Eustace more in love than ever.

But Winifred?

One afternoon she sat in the drawing-room of the pretty little house they had taken in Deanery Street, Park Lane. She was thinking, very definitely. The silent processes of even an ordinary woman's mind—what great male writer would not give two years of his life to sit with them and watch them, as the poet watches the flight of a swallow, or the astronomer the processions of the sky? A curious gale was raging through the town, touzling its thatch of chimney-pots, doing violence to the demureness of its respectable streets. Night was falling, and in Piccadilly those strange, gay hats that greet the darkness were coming out like eager, vulgar comets in a dim and muttering firmament. It was just the moment when the outside mood of the huge city begins to undergo a change, to glide from its comparative simplicity of afternoon into its leering complexity of evening. Each twenty-four hours London has its moment of emancipation, its moment in which the wicked begin to breathe and the good to wonder, when " How?" and "Why?" are on the lips of the opposing fac-

tions, and only the philosophers who know—
or think they know—their human nature hold
themselves still, and feel that man is at the
least ceaselessly interesting.

Winifred sat by the fire and held a council.
She called her thoughts together and gave
audience to her suspicions, and her brown
eyes were wide and rather mournful as her
counsellors uttered each a word of hope or
of warning.

Eustace was out.   He had gone to a concert, and had not returned.

She was holding a council to decide something in reference to him.

The honeymoon weeks had brought her
just as far as the question, " Do I know
my husband at all, or is he, so far, a total
stranger ? "

Some people seem to draw near to you as
you look at them steadily, others to recede
until they reach the verge of invisibility.
Which was Eustace doing ? Did his outline
become clearer or more blurred ? Was he
daily more definite or more phantasmal ?
And the members of her council drew near
and whispered their opinions in Winifred's
attentive ears. They were not all in accord
at the first. Pros fought with cons, elbowed
them, were hustled in return.   Sometimes

there was almost a row, and she had to stretch forth her hands and hush the tumult. For she desired a calm conclave, although she was a woman.

And the final decision—if, indeed, it could be arrived at that evening—was important. Love seemed to hang upon it, and all the sweets of life; and the little wings of Love fluttered anxiously, as the little wings of a bird flutter when you hold it in the cage of your hands, prisoning it from its wayward career through the blue shadows of the summer.

For love is not always and for ever instinctive—not even the finest love. While many women love because they must, whether the thing to be loved or not loved be carrion or crystal, a child of the gods or an imp of the devil, others love decisively because they see—perhaps can even analyze—a beauty that is there in the thing before them. One woman loves a man simply because he kisses her. Another loves him because he has won the Victoria Cross.

Winifred was not of the women who love because they are kissed.

She had accepted Eustace rather impulsively, but she had not married him quite uncritically. There was something new, differ-

ent from other men, about him which at-
tracted her, as well as his good looks—that
prettiness which had peeped out from the
white wig in the scarlet nook at the ball.
His oddities at that time she had grown
thoroughly to believe in, and, believing in
them, she felt she liked them. She supposed
them to spring, rather like amazing spotted
orchids, from the earth of a quaint nature.
Now, after a honeymoon spent among the
orchids, she held this council while the wind
blew London into a mood of evening irritation.

What was Eustace?

How the wind sang over Park Lane! Yet
the stars were coming out.

What was he? A genius or a clown? A
creature to spread a buttered slide or a man
to climb to heaven? A fine, free child of
Nature, who did, freshly, what he would, re-
gardless of the strained discretion of others,
or a futile, scheming hypocrite, screaming
after forced puerilities, without even a finger
on the skirts of originality?

It was a problem for lonely woman's de-
bate. Winifred strove to weigh it well. In
Bluebeard's Chamber Eustace had cut many
capers. This activity she had expected—had
even wished for. And at first she had been

amused and entertained by the antics, as one assisting at a good burlesque, through which, moreover, a piquant love theme runs. But by degrees she began to feel a certain stiffness in the capers, a self-consciousness in the antics, or fancied she began to feel it, and instead of being always amused she became often thoughtful.

Whimsicality she loved. Buffoonery she possibly, even probably, could learn to hate.

Of Eustace's love for her she had no doubt. She was certain of his affection. But was it worth having? That depended, surely, on the nature of the man in whom it sprang, from whom it flowed. She wanted to be sure of that nature; but she acknowledged to herself, as she sat by the fire, that she was perplexed. Perhaps even that perplexity was merciful. Yet she wished to sweep it away. She knit her brows moodily, and longed for a secret divining-rod that would twist to reveal truth in another. For truth, she thought, is better than hidden water-springs, and a sincerity—even of stupidity—more lovely than the fountain that gives flowers to the desert, wild red roses to the weary gold of sands.

The wind roared again, howling to poor, shuddering Mayfair, and there came a step outside. Eustace sprang in upon Winifred's council, looking like a gay schoolboy, his cheeks flushed, his lips open to speak.

" Dreaming ? " he said.

She smiled.

" Perhaps."

" That concert paralyzed me. Too much Beethoven. I wanted Wagner. Beethoven insists on exalting you, but Wagner lets you revel and feel naughty. Winnie, d'you hear the wind ? "

" Could I help it ? " she asked.

" Does it suggest something to you ? "

He looked at her, and made his expression mischievous, or meant to make it. She looked up at him, too.

" Yes, many things," she said—" many, many things."

" To me it suggests kites."

" Kites ? "

" Yes. I'm going to fly one now in the Park. The stars are out. Put on your hat and come with me."

He seemed all impulse, sparkling to the novelty of the idea.

" Well, but——" She hesitated.

" I've got one—a beauty, a monster ! I noticed the wind was getting up yesterday. Come ! "

He pulled at her hand ; she obeyed him,

not quickly. She put on her hat, a plain straw, a thick jacket, gloves. Kite-flying in London seemed an odd notion. Was it lively and entertaining, or merely silly? Which ought it to be?

Eustace shouted to her from the tiny hall. "Hurry!" he cried.

The wind yelled beyond the door, and Winifred ran down, beginning to feel a childish thrill of excitement. Eustace held the kite. It was, indeed, a white monster, gaily decorated with fluttering scarlet and blue ribbons.

"We shall be mobbed," she said.

"There's no one about," he answered. "The gale frightens people."

He opened the door, and they were out in the crying tempest. The great clouds flew along the sky like an army in retreat. Some, to Winifred, seemed soldiers, others baggage-waggons, horses, gun-carriages, rushing pell-mell for safety. One drooping, tattered cloud she deemed the colours of a regiment streaming under the stars that peeped out here and there—watching sentinel eyes, obdurate, till some magic password softened them.

As they crossed the road she spoke of her cloud army to Eustace.

3

"This kite's like a live thing," was his
reply. "It tugs as a fish tugs a line."

He did not care for the tumult of a far-
off world.

They entered the Park. It seemed, indeed, strangely deserted. A swaggering soldier passed them by, going towards the Marble Arch. His spurs clinked; his long cloak
gleamed like a huge pink carnation in the
dingy dimness of the startled night. How
he stared with his unintelligent, though bold,
eyes as he saw the kite bounding to be free.

Eustace seemed delighted.

"That man thinks us mad!" he said.

"Are we mad?" Winifred asked, surprised
at her own strange enjoyment of the adventure.

"Who knows?" said Eustace, looking at
her narrowly. "You like this escapade?"

"Yes," she answered.

"My mask!" he thought, secretly longing to be quietly by the fire sipping tea and
reading *Punch*. "She loves that."

They were through the trees now, across
the broad path, out on the open lawns.

"Now for it!" he shouted, as the wind
roared in their faces.

He paid out the coils of the thin cord.
The white monster skimmed, struggled near

the ground, returned, darted again upward
and outward, felt for the wind's hands, caught
them and sprang, with a mad courage, star-
wards, its gay ribbons flying like coloured
birds to mark its course. But soon they were
lost to sight, and only a diminished, ghost-like
shadow leaping against the black showed
where the kite beat on to liberty.

Eustace ran with the wind, and Winifred
followed him. The motion sent an exulta-
tion dancing through her veins, and stirred
her blood into a ferment. The noises in the
trees, the galloping music of the airs on their
headlong courses, rang in her ears like clash-
ing bells. She called as she ran, but never
knew what words. She leaped, as if over
glorious obstacles. Her feet danced on the
short grass. She had a sudden notion: " I
am living now!" and Eustace had never
seemed so near to her. He had an art to find
why children are happy, she thought, because
they do little strange things, coupling mechanical movements, obvious actions that
may seem absurd, with soft flights of the
imagination, that wrap their prancings and
their leaps in golden robes, and give to the
dull world a glory. The hoop is their demon
enemy, whom they drive before them to destruction. The kite is a great white bird,

whom they hold back for a time from heaven. Suddenly Winifred longed to feel the bird's efforts to be free.

"Let me have it!" she cried to Eustace, holding out her hands eagerly. "Do let me!"

He was glad to pass the cord to her, being utterly tired of a prank which he thought idiotic, and he could not understand the light that sprang into her eyes as she grasped it, and felt the life of the lifeless thing that soared towards the clouds.

For the moment it was more to her—this tugging, scarce visible, white thing—than all the world of souls. It gave to her the excitement of battle, the joy of strife. She felt herself a Napoleon with empires in her hand; a Diana holding eternities, instead of hounds, in leash. She had quite the children's idea of kites, the sense of being in touch with the infinite that enters into baby pleasures, and makes the remembrance of them live in us when we are old, and have forgotten wild passions, strange fruitions, that have followed them and faded away for ever.

How the creature tore at her! She fancied she felt the pulsings of its fly-away heart, beating with energy and great hopes of freedom. And suddenly, with a call, she opened her hands. Her captive was lost in the night.

In a moment she felt sad, such a foolish sorrow, as a gaoler may feel sad who has grown to love his prisoner, and sees him smile when the gaping door gives him again to crime.

"It's gone," she said to Eustace; "I think it's glad to go."

"Glad—a kite!" he said.

And it struck her that he would have thought it equally sensible if she had spoken, like Hans Andersen, of the tragedies of a toy-shop or the Homeric passions of wooden dolls.

Then, why had he been prompted by the wind to play the boy if he had none of the boy's ardent imagination?

They reached Deanery Street, and passed in from the night and the elements. Eustace shut the door with a sigh of relief. Winifred's echoing sigh was of regret.

It seemed a listless world—the world inside a lighted London house, dominated by a pale butler with black side-whiskers and endless discretion. But Eustace did not feel it so. Winifred knew that beyond hope of doubt as she stole a glance at his face. He had put off the child—the buffoon—and looked for the moment a grave, dull young man, naturally at ease with all the conventions.   She could not help saying to herself, as she went to her room to live with hairpins and her lady's-maid : "I believe he hated it all!"

From that night of kite-flying Winifred felt differently towards her husband. She was of the comparatively rare women who hate pretence even in another woman, but especially in a man. The really eccentric she was not afraid of—could even love, being a searcher after the new and strange, like so many modern pilgrims. But pinchbeck eccentricity—Brummagem originalities—gave to her views of the poverty of poor human nature leading her to a depression not untinged with contempt.

And the fantasies of Eustace became more violent and more continuous as he began to note the lassitude which gradually crept into her intercourse with him. London rang with them. At one time he pretended to a strange passion for death ; prayed to a skull which grinned in a shrine raised for it in his dressing-room ; lay down each day in a coffin, and asked Winifred to close it and scatter earth upon the lid, that he might realize the end towards which we journey. He talked of silence, long and loudly—an irony which Winifred duly noted—sneered at the fleeting phantoms in the show of existence, called the sobbing of women, the laughter of men, sounds as arid as the whizz of a cracker let off by a child on the fifth of November.

"We should kill our feelings," he said. "They make us absurd. Life should be a breathing calm, as death is a breathless calm."

The calm descending upon Winifred was of the benumbing order.

Later he recoiled from this coquetting with the destroyer.

"After all," he said, "which of us does not feel himself eternal, exempt from the penalty of the race? You don't believe that you will ever die, Winifred?"

"I know it," she said.

"Yes, but you don't believe it."

"You think knowledge less real than belief? Perhaps it is. But I, at least, hope that some day I shall die. To live on here for ever would be like staying eternally at a party. After all, when one has danced, and supped, and flirted, and wondered at the gowns, and praised the flowers, and touched the hand of one's hostess, and swung round in a final gallop, and said how much one has enjoyed it all—one wants to go home."

"Does one?" Eustace said. "Home you call it!"

He shuddered.

"I call it what I want it to be, what I think it may be, what the poor and the weary and the fallen make it in their lonely thoughts. Let us, at least, hope that we travel towards the east, where the sun is."

"You have strange fancies," he said.

"I! Not so strange as yours."

She looked at him in the eyes as she spoke. He wondered what that look meant. It seemed to him a menace.

"I must keep it up—I must keep it up," he murmured to himself as he left the room. "Winifred loves fancies—loves me for what she thinks mine."

He went to his library, and sat down heavily, to devise fresh outrages on the ordinary.

His pranks became innumerable, and Society called him the most original figure of London. The papers quoted him—his doings, not his sayings. People pointed him out in the Park. His celebrity waxed. Even the Marble Arch seemed turning to gaze after him as he went by, showing the observation which the imaginative think into inanimate things.

At least, so a wag declared.

And Winifred bore it, but with an increasing impatience.

At this time, too, a strange need of protection crept over her, the yearning for man's beautiful, dog-like sympathy that watches woman in her grand dark hour before she blooms into motherhood. When she knew the truth, she resolved to tell Eustace, and she came into his room softly, with shining eyes. He was sitting reading the *Financial News* in a nimbus of cigarette smoke, secretly glorying in his momentary immunity from the prison rules of the fantastic. Winifred's entry was as that of a warder. He sprang up laughing.

"Winnie," he said, "I think I am going to South Africa."

"You!" she said in surprise.

"Yes; to give acrobatic performances in the street, and so pave the way to a position as a millionaire. Who ever heard of a man rising from a respectable competence to a fortune? According to the papers, you must start with nothing; that is the first rule of the game. We have ten thousand a year, so we can never hope to be rich. Fortune only favours the pauper. I am mad about money to-day. I can think of nothing else."

And he began showing her conjuring tricks with sovereigns which he drew from his pockets.

She did not tell him that day. And when she told him, it was without apparent emotion. She seemed merely stating coldly a physical fact, not breathing out a beautiful secret of her soul and his, a consecrated wonder to shake them both, and bind them together as two flowers are bound in the centre of a bouquet, the envy of the other flowers.

"Eustace," she said, and her eyes were clear and her hands were still, "I think I ought to tell you—we shall have a child."

Her voice was unwavering as a doctor's which pronounces, " You have the influenza." She stood there before him.

"Winifred!" he cried, looking up. His impulse was to say, " Wife! My Winifred!" to take her in his arms as any clerk might take his little middle-class spouse, to kiss her lips, and, in doing it, fancy he drew near to the prison in which every soul eternally dwells on earth. Finely human he felt, as the dullest, the most unknown, the plainest, the most despised, may feel, thank God! " Winifred!" he cried. And then he stopped, with the shooting thought, "Even now I must be what she thinks me, what she perhaps loves me for."

She stood there silently waiting.

"Toys!" he exclaimed. "Toys have always been my besetting sin. Now I will make a grand collection, not for the Pope, as people pretend, but for our family. You will have two children to laugh at, Winnie. Your husband is one, you know." He sprang up. "I'll go into the Strand," he said. "There's a man near the Temple who has always got some delightful novelty displaying its paces on the pavement. What fun!"

And off he went, leaving Winifred alone with the mystery of her woman's world, the mystic mystery of birth that may dawn out of hate as out of love, out of drunken dissipation as out of purity's sweet climax.

Next day a paragraph in the papers told how Mr. Eustace Lane had bought up all the penny toys of the Strand. Mention was again made of his supposed mission to the Vatican, and a picture drawn of the bewilderment of the Holy Father, roused from contemplation of the eternal to contemplation of jumping pasteboard, and the frigid gestures of people from the world of *papier-maché*.

Eustace showed the paragraph to Winifred.

"Why will they chronicle all I do?" he said, with a sigh.

"Would you rather they did not?"

"Oh, if it amuses them," he answered. "To amuse the world is to be its bene-factor."

"No, to comfort the world," was Wini-fred's silent thought.

To her the world often seemed a weary invalid, playing cards on the coverlet of the bed from which it longed in vain to move, peeping with heavy eyes at the shrouded windows of its chamber, and listening for faint sounds from without—soft songs, soft murmurings, the breath of winds, the sigh of showers; then turning with a smothered groan to its cards again, its lengthy game of "Patience." Clubs, spades, hearts, diamonds —there they all lay on the coverlet ready to the hands of the invalid. But she wanted to take them away, and give to the sufferer a prayer and a hope.

At this period she was often full of a vague, chaotic tenderness, far-reaching, yet indefinite. She could rather have kissed the race than a person.

And so the days went by, Winifred in a dream of wonder, Eustace in the toy-shops.

Until the birthday dawned and faded.

All through that day Eustace was in agony. He did not care so much for the child, but he loved the mother. Her danger tore at his heart. Her pain smote him, till he seemed to feel it actually and physically. That she was giving him something was naught to him; that she might be taken away in the giving was everything. And when he learnt that all was well, he cried and prayed, and thought to himself afterwards, " If Winifred could know what I am like, what I have done to-day, how would it strike her?"

She did not know; for when at length Eustace was admitted to her room, he trained himself to murmur, " A girl, that's lucky because of all the dolls. The Pope sha'n't have even one now."

Winifred lay back white on her pillow, and a little frown travelled across her face. If Eustace had just kissed her, and she had felt a tear of his on her face, and he had said nothing, she could have loved him then as a father, perhaps, more than as a husband. His allusion to the supposed Papal absurdity disgusted her at such a time, only faintly, because of her weakness, but distinctly, and in a way to be remembered.

She recovered: but just as the child was beginning to smile, and to express an approbation of life by murmurous gurglings, an infantile disease gripped it, held it, would not release it. And Winifred knelt beside it, dead, and thought, with a new and vital horror, of the invalid world playing cards upon the drawn coverlet of its bed. Baby was outside that chamber now, beyond the curtained windows, outside in sun or shower that she could not see, could only dream of, while the game of " Patience " went on and on.

III.

THE death of the child meant more to Winifred than she would at first acknowledge even to herself. Almost unconsciously she had looked forward to its birth as to a release from bondage. There are moments when a duet is gaol, a trio comparative liberty. The child, the tiny intruder into youthful married life, may come in the guise of an imp or of a good fairy : one to cloud the perfect and complete joy of two, or one to give sunlight to their nascent weariness and dissatisfaction. Or, again, it may be looked for with longing by one of two lovers, with apprehension by the other. Only when it lay dead did Winifred understand that Eustace was to her a stranger, and that she was lonely alone with him. The "Au revoir" of two bodies may be sweet, but the "Au revoir" of two minds is generally but a hypocritical or sarcastic rendering of the tragic word "Adieu." Winifred's mind cried "Au revoir" to the mind of Eustace, to his nature, to his love, but deep in her soul trembled the minor music, the shuddering discord, of "Adieu." Adieu to the body of child; adieu more complete, more eternal, to the soul of husband. Which good bye was the stranger? She stood as at cross-roads, and watched, with hand-shaded eyes, the tiny, wayward babe dwindling on its journey to heaven; the man she had married dwindling on his journey—whither? And the one she had a full hope of meeting again, but the other——

After the funeral the Lanes took up once more the old dual life which had been momentarily interrupted. Had it not been for the interruption, Winifred fancied that she might not have awakened to the full knowledge of her own feelings towards Eustace until a much later period. But the baby's birth, existence, passing away, were a blow upon the gate of life from the vague without. She had opened the gate, caught a glimpse of the shadowy land of the possible. And to do that is often to realize in a flash the impossibility of one's individual fate. So many of us manage to live ignorantly all our days and to call ourselves happy. Winifred could never live quite ignorantly again.

To Eustace the interruption meant much less. So long as he had Winifred he could not feel that any of his dreams hung altogether in tatters. Sometimes, it is true, he contemplated the penny toys, and had a moment of quaint, not unpleasant regret, half forming the thought, Why do we ever trouble ourselves to prepare happiness for others, when happiness is a word of a thousand meanings? As often as not, to do so is to set a dinner of many courses and many wines before an unknown guest, who proves to be vegetarian and teetotaler, after all.

"What shall I do with the toys?" he asked Winifred one day.

"The toys? Oh, give them to a children's hospital," she said, and her voice had a harsh note in it.

"No," he answered, after a moment's reflection; "I'll keep them and play with them myself; you know I love toys."

And on the following Sunday, when many callers came to Deanery Street, they found him in the drawing-room, playing with a Noah's ark. Red, green, violet, and azure elephants, antelopes, zebras, and pigs processed along the carpet, guided by an orange-coloured Noah in a purple top-hat, and a perfect parterre of sons and wives. The fixed anxiety of their painted faces suggested that they were in apprehension of the flood, but their rigid attitudes implied trust in the Unseen.

Winifred's face that day seemed changed to those who knew her best. To one man, a soldier who had admired her greatly before her marriage, and who had seen no reason to change his opinion of her since, she was more cordial than usual, and he went away curiously meditating on the mystery of women.

"What has happened to Mrs. Lane?" he thought to himself as he walked down Park Lane. "That last look of hers at me, when I was by the door, going, was—yes, I'll swear it—Regent Street. And yet Winnie Lane is the purest—I'm hanged if I can make out women! Anyhow, I'll go there again. People say she and that fantastic ass she's married are devoted. H'm!" He went to Pall Mall, and sat staring at nothing in his Club till seven, deep in the mystery of the female sex.

And he went again to Deanery Street to see whether the vision of Regent Street was deceptive, and came away wondering and hoping. From this time the vagaries of Eustace Lane became more incessant, more flamboyant, than ever, and Mrs. Lane was perpetually in society. If it would not have been true to say, conventionally, that no party was complete without her, yet it certainly seemed, from this time, that she was incomplete without a party. She was the starving wolf after the sledge in which sat the gay world. If the sledge escaped her, she was left to face darkness, snow, wintry winds, loneliness. In London do we not often hear the dismal howling of the wolves, suggesting steppes of the heart frigid as Siberia?

Eustace grew uneasy, for Winifred seemed eluding him in this maze of entertainments. He could not impress the personality of his mask upon her vitally when she moved perpetually in the pantomime processions of society, surrounded by grotesques, mimes, dancers, and deformities.

"We are scarcely ever alone, Winnie," he said to her one day.

"You must learn to love me in a crowd," she answered. "Human nature can love even God in isolation, but the man who can love God in the world is the true Christian."

"I can love you anywhere," he said. "But

you——" And then he stopped and quickly readjusted his mask which was slipping off.

From that day he monotonously accentuated his absurdities. All London rang with them. He was the Court Fool of Mayfair, the buffoon of the inner circles of the Metropolis, and, by degrees, his painted fame, jangling the bells in its cap, spun about England in a dervish dance, till Peckham whispered of him, and even the remotest suburbs crowned him with parsley and hung upon his doings. All the blooming flowers of notoriety were his, to hug in his arms as he stood upon his platform bowing to the general applause. His shrine in *Vanity Fair* was surely being prepared. But he scarcely thought of this, being that ordinary, ridiculous, middle-class thing, an immoderately loving husband, insane enough to worship romantically the woman to whom he was unromantically tied by the law of his country. With each new fantasy he hoped to win back that which he had lost. Each joke was the throw of a desperate gamester, each tricky invention a stake placed on the number that would never turn up. That wild time of his career was humorous to the world, how tragic to himself we can only wonder. He spread wings like a bird, flew hither and thither as if a vagrant for pure joy and the pleasure of movement, darted and poised, circled and sailed, but all the time his heart cried aloud for a nest and Winifred. Yet he wooed her only silently by his follies, and set her each day farther and farther from him.

And she—how she hated his notoriety, and was sick with weariness when voices told her of his escapades, modulating themselves to wondering praise. Long ago she had known that Eustace sinned against his own nature, but she had never loved him quite enough to discover what that nature really was. And now she had no desire to find out. He was only her husband and the least of all men to her.

.   .   .   .   .   .

The Lanes sat at breakfast one morning and took up their letters. Winifred sipped her tea, and opened one or two carelessly. They were invitations. Then she tore the envelope of a third, and, as she read it, forgot to sip her tea. Presently she laid it down slowly. Eustace was looking at her.

"Winifred," he said, "I have got a letter from the editor of *Vanity Fair.*"

"Oh!"

"He wishes me to permit a caricature of myself to appear in his pages."

Winifred's fingers closed sharply on the letter she had just been reading. A decision of hers in regard to the writer of it was hanging in the balance, though Eustace did not know it.

"Well?" said Eustace, inquiring of her silence.

"What are you going to reply?" she asked.

"I am wondering."

She chipped an eggshell and took a bit of dry toast.

"All those who appear in *Vanity Fair* are celebrated, aren't they?" she said.

"I suppose so," Eustace said.

"For many different things."

"Of course."

"Can you refuse the editor's request?"

"I don't know why I should."

"Exactly. Tell me when you have written to him, and what you have written, Eustace."

"Yes, Winnie, I will."

Later on in the day he came up to her boudoir, and said to her:

"I have told him I am quite willing to have my caricature in his paper."

"Your portrait," she said. "All right. Leave me now, Eustace; I have some writing to do."

As soon as he had gone she sat down and wrote a short letter, which she posted herself.

A month later Eustace came bounding up the stairs to find her.

"Winnie, Winnie!" he called. "Where are you? I've something to show you."

He held a newspaper in his hand. Winifred was not in the room. Eustace rang the bell.

"Where is Mrs. Lane?" he asked of the footman who answered it.

"Gone out, sir," the man answered.

"And not back yet? It's very late," said Eustace, looking at his watch.

The time was a quarter to eight. They were dining at half-past.

"I wonder where she is," he thought.

Then he sat down and gazed at a cartoon which represented a thin man with a preternaturally pale face, legs like sticks, and drooping hands full of toys—himself. Beneath it was written, "His aim is to amuse."

He turned a page, and read, for the third or fourth time, the following:

"MR. EUSTACE LANE.

"Mr. Eustace Bernhard Lane, only son of Mr. Merton Lane, of Carlton House Terrace, was born in London twenty-eight years ago. He is married to one of the belles of the daÿ, and is probably the most envied husband in town.

"Although he is such a noted figure in society, Mr. Eustace Lane has never done any conspicuously good or bad deed.. He has neither invented a bicycle nor written a novel, neither lost a seat in Parliament, nor found a mine in South Africa. Careless of elevating the world, he has been content to entertain it, to make it laugh, or to make it wonder. His aim is to amuse, and his whole-souled endeavour to succeed in this ambition has gained him the entire respect of the frivolous. What more could man desire?"

As he finished there came a ring at the hall-door bell.

"Winifred!" he exclaimed, and jumped up with the paper in his hand.

In a moment the footman entered with a note.

"A boy messenger has just brought this, sir," he said.

Eustace took it, and, as the man went out and shut the door, opened it, and read:

"VICTORIA STATION.

"This is to say good-bye. By the time it

reaches you I shall have left London. Not
alone. I have seen the cartoon. It is very
like you. WINIFRED."

Eustace sank down in a chair.

On the table at his elbow lay *Vanity Fair*.
Mechanically he looked at it, and read once
more the words beneath his picture, "His
aim is to amuse."

THE RETURN OF THE SOUL.

" I have been here before,
But when, or how, I cannot tell ! "

ROSSETTI.

I.

TUESDAY NIGHT, *November 3rd.*

THEORIES ! What is the good of theories ?
They are the scourges that lash our minds in
modern days, lash them into confusion, perplexity, despair. I have never been troubled
by them before. Why should I be troubled
by them now ? And the absurdity of Profess-
or Black's is surely obvious. A child would
laugh at it. Yes, a child ! I have never been
a diary writer. I have never been able to understand the amusement of sitting down late
at night and scrawling minutely in some hidden book every paltry incident of one's paltry
days. People say it is so interesting to read
the entries years afterwards. To read, as a
man, the *menu* that I ate through as a boy,
the love-story that I was actor in, the tragedy
that I brought about, the debt that I have

never paid—how could it profit me? To keep a diary has always seemed to me merely an addition to the ills of life. Yet now I have a hidden book, like the rest of the world, and I am scrawling in it to-day. Yes, but for a reason.

I want to make things clear to myself, and I find, as others, that my mind works more easily with the assistance of the pen. The actual tracing of words on paper dispels the clouds that cluster round my thoughts. I shall recall events to set my mind at ease, to prove to myself how absurd a man who could believe in Professor Black would be. "Little Dry-as-dust" I used to call him. Dry? He is full of wild romance, rubbish that a school-girl would be ashamed to believe in. Yet he is abnormally clever; his record proves that. Still, clever men are the first to be led astray, they say. It is the searcher who follows the wandering light. What he says can't be true. When I have filled these pages, and read what I have written dispassionately, as one of the outside public might read, I shall have done, once for all, with the ridiculous fancies that are beginning to make my life a burden. To put my thoughts in order will make a music. The evil spirit within me will sleep, will die. I

shall be cured.   It must be so — it shall
be so.

To go back to the beginning.   Ah! what
a long time ago that seems!   As a child I was
cruel.   Most boys are cruel, I think. My
school companions were a merciless set—merciless to one another, to their masters when
they had a chance, to animals, to birds.   The
desire to torture was in nearly all of them.
They loved to bully, and if they bullied only
mildly, it was from fear, not from love.   They
did not wish their boomerang to return and
slay them.   If a boy were deformed, they
twitted him.   If a master were kind, or gentle, or shy, they made his life as intolerable
as they could.   If an animal or a bird came
into their power, they had no pity.   I was like
the rest; indeed, I think that I was worse.
Cruelty is horrible.   I have enough imagination to do more than know that—to feel it.

Some say that it is lack of imagination
which makes men and women brutes.   May
it not be power of imagination?   The interest of torturing is lessened, is almost lost, if
we can not be the tortured as well as the tor-
turer.

As a child I was cruel by nature, by instinct.   I was a handsome, well-bred, gentle-
manlike, gentle-looking little brute.   My par-

ents adored me, and I was good to them. They were so kind to me that I was almost fond of them. Why not? It seemed to me as politic to be fond of them as of anyone else. I did what I pleased, but I did not always let them know it; so I pleased them. The wise child will take care to foster the ignorance of its parents. My people were pretty well off, and I was their only child; but my chief chances of future pleasure in life were centred in my grandmother, my mother's mother. She was immensely rich, and she lived here. This room in which I am writing now was her favourite sitting-room. On that hearth, before a log fire, such as is burning at this moment, used to sit that wonderful cat of hers—that horrible cat! Why did I ever play my childish cards to win this house, this place? Sometimes, lately—very lately only—I have wondered, like a fool perhaps. Yet would Professor Black say so? I remember, as a boy of sixteen, paying my last visit here to my grandmother. It bored me very much to come. But she was said to be near death, and death leaves great houses vacant for others to fill. So when my mother said that I had better come, and my father added that he thought my grandmother was fonder of me than of my other relations, I gave up all my

boyish plans for the holidays with apparent
willingness. Though almost a child, I was
not short-sighted. I knew every boy had a
future as well as a present. I gave up my
plans, and came here with a smile; but in my
heart I hated my grandmother for having
power, and so bending me to relinquish pleasure for boredom. I hated her, and I came to
her and kissed her, and saw her beautiful
white Persian cat sitting before the fire in this
room, and thought of the fellow who was my
bosom friend, and with whom I longed to be,
shooting, or fishing, or riding. And I looked
at the cat again. I remember it began to
purr when I went near to it. It sat quite still,
with its blue eyes fixed upon the fire, but when
I approached it I heard it purr complacently.
I longed to kick it. The limitations of its
ridiculous life satisfied it completely. It
seemed to reproduce in an absurd, diminished
way my grandmother in her white lace cap,
with her white face and hands. She sat in
her chair all day and looked at the fire. The
cat sat on the hearthrug and did the same.
The cat seemed to me the animal personification of the human being who kept me chained
from all the sports and pleasures I had prom-
ised myself for the holidays. When I went
near to the cat, and heard it calmly purring

at me, I longed to do it an injury. It seemed
to me as if it understood what my grandmother did not, and was complacently tri-
umphing at my voluntary imprisonment with
age, and laughing to itself at the pains men—
and boys—will undergo for the sake of money.
Brute! I did not love my grandmother, and
she had money. I hated the cat utterly. It
hadn't a *sou!*

This beautiful house is not old. My
grandfather built it himself. He had no love
for the life of towns, I believe, but was passionately in touch with nature, and, when a
young man, he set out on a strange tour
through England. His object was to find a
perfect view, and in front of that view he in-
tended to build himself a habitation. For
nearly a year, so I have been told, he wan-
dered through Scotland and England, and at
last he came to this place in Cumberland, to
this village, to this very spot. Here his wan-
derings ceased. Standing on the terrace—
then uncultivated forest—that runs in front
of these windows, he found at last what he
desired. He bought the forest. He bought
the windings of the river, the fields upon its
banks, and on the extreme edge of the steep
gorge through which it runs he built the lovely dwelling that to-day is mine.

This place is no ordinary place. It is characteristic in the highest degree. The house is wonderfully situated, with the ground falling abruptly in front of it, the river forming almost a horseshoe round it. The woods are lovely. The garden, curiously, almost wildly, laid out, is like no other garden I ever saw. And the house, though not old, is full of little surprises, curiously shaped rooms, remarkable staircases, quaint recesses. The place is a place to remember. The house is a house to fix itself in the memory. Nothing that had once lived here could ever come back and forget that it had been here. Not even an animal—not even an animal.

I wish I had never gone to that dinner-party and met the Professor. There was a horror coming upon me then. He has hastened its steps. He has put my fears into shape, my vague wondering into words. Why cannot men leave life alone? Why will they catch it by the throat and wring its secrets from it? To respect reserve is one of the first instincts of the gentleman; and life is full of reserve.

It is getting very late. I thought I heard a step in the house just now. I wonder—I wonder if *she* is asleep. I wish I knew.

Day after day passed by. My grandmother seemed to be failing, but almost imperceptibly. She evidently loved to have me near to her. Like most old dying people, in her mind she frantically clutched at life, that could give to her nothing more; and I believe she grew to regard me as the personification of all that was leaving her. My vitality warmed her. She extended her hands to my flaming hearthfire. She seemed trying to live in my life, and at length became afraid to let me out of her sight. One day she said to me, in her quavering, ugly voice—old voices are so ugly, like hideous echoes:

"Ronald, I could never die while you were in the room. So long as you are with me, where I can touch you, I shall live."

And she put out her white, corrugated hand, and fondled my warm boy's hand.

How I longed to push her hand away, and get out into the sunlight and the air, and hear young voices, the voices of the morning, not of the twilight, and be away from wrinkled Death, that seemed sitting on the doorstep of that house huddled up like a beggar, waiting for the door to be opened!

I was bored till I grew malignant. I confess it. And, feeling malignant, I began to long more and more passionately to vent myself on someone or something. I looked at

the cat, which, as usual, was sitting before
the fire.

Animals have intuitions as keen as those
of a woman, keener than those of a man.
They inherit an instinct of fear of those who
hate them from a long line of ancestors who
have suffered at the hands of cruel men.
They can tell by a look, by a motion, by the
tone of a voice, whether to expect from anyone kindness or malignity. The cat had
purred complacently on the first day of my
arrival, and had hunched up her white, furry
back towards my hand, and had smiled with
her calm, light-blue eyes. Now, when I approached her, she seemed to gather herself
together and to make herself small. She
shrank from me. There was—as I fancied—
a dawning comprehension, a dawning terror
in her blue eyes. She always sat very close
to my grandmother now, as if she sought protection, and she watched me as if she were
watching for an intention which she appre-
hended to grow in my mind.

And the intention came.

For, as the days went on, and my grandmother still lived, I began to grow desperate.
My holiday time was over now, but my parents wrote telling me to stay where I was,
and not to think of returning to school. My

5

grandmother had caused a letter to be sent
to them in which she said that she could not
part from me, and added that my parents
would never have cause to regret interrupting
my education for a time. "He will be paid
in full for every moment he loses," she wrote,
referring to me.

It seemed a strange taste in her to care
so much for a boy, but she had never loved
women, and I was handsome, and she liked
handsome faces. The brutality in my nature was not written upon my features. I
had smiling, frank brown eyes, a lithe young
figure, a gay boy's voice. My movements
were quick, and I have always been told that
my gestures were never awkward, my demeanour was never unfinished, as is the case so
often with lads at school. Outwardly I was
attractive; and the old woman, who had
married two husbands merely for their looks,
delighted in feeling that she had the power
to retain me by her side at an age when most
boys avoid old people as if they were the
pestilence.

And then I pretended to love her, and
obeyed all her insufferably tiresome behests.
But I longed to wreak vengeance upon her
all the same. My dearest friend, the fellow
with whom I was to have spent my holidays,

was leaving at the end of this term which I
was missing. He wrote to me furious letters,
urging me to come back, and reproaching me
for my selfishness and lack of affection.

Each time I received one I looked at the
cat, and the cat shrank nearer to my grandmother's chair.

It never purred now, and nothing would
induce it to leave the room where she sat.
One day the servant said to me:

"I believe the poor dumb thing knows
my mistress can't last very much longer, sir.
The way that cat looks up at her goes to my
heart. Ah! them beasts understand things as
well as we do, I believe."

I think the cat understood quite well. It
did watch my grandmother in a very strange
way, gazing up into her face, as if to mark
the changing contours, the increasing lines,
the down-droop of the features, that bespoke
the gradual soft approach of death. It listened to the sound of her voice; and as, each
day, the voice grew more vague, more weak
and toneless, an anxiety that made me exult
dawned and deepened in its blue eyes. Or so
I thought.

I had a great deal of morbid imagination
at that age, and loved to weave a web of fancies, mostly horrible, around almost every-

thing that entered into my life. It pleased
me to believe that the cat understood each
new intention that came into my mind, read
me silently from its place near the fire, tracked
my thoughts, and was terror-stricken as they
concentrated themselves round a definite resolve, which hardened and toughened day by
day.

It pleased me to believe, do I say? I did
really believe, and do believe now, that the
cat understood all, and grew haggard with
fear as my grandmother failed visibly. For
it knew what the end would mean for it.

That first day of my arrival, when I saw
my grandmother in her white cap, with her
white face and hands, and the big white cat
sitting near to her, I had thought there was a
similarity between them. That similarity
struck me more forcibly, grew upon me, as
my time in the house grew longer, until the
latter seemed almost a reproduction of the
former, and after each letter from my friend
my hate for the two increased. But my hate
for my grandmother was impotent, and would
always be so. I could never repay her for
the *ennui*, the furious, forced inactivity which
made my life a burden, and spurred my bad
passions while they lulled me in a terrible,
enforced repose. I could repay her favour-

ite, the thing she had always cherished, her feline confidant, who lived in safety under the shadow of her protection. I could wreak my fury on that when the protection was withdrawn, as it must be at last. It seemed to my brutal, imaginative, unfinished boy's mind that the murder of her pet must hurt and wound my grandmother even after she was dead. I would make her suffer then, when she was impotent to wreak a vengeance upon me. I would kill the cat.

The creature knew my resolve the day I made it, and had even, I should say, anticipated it.

As I sat day after day beside my grandmother's armchair in the dim room, with the blinds drawn to shut out the summer sunlight, and talked to her in a subdued and reverent voice, agreeing with all the old banalities she uttered, all the preposterous opinions she propounded, all the commands she laid upon me, I gazed beyond her at the cat, and the creature was haggard with apprehension.

It knew, as I knew, that its day was coming. Sometimes I bent down and took it up on my lap to please my grandmother, and praised its beauty and its gentleness to her. And all the time I felt its warm, furry body trembling with horror between my hands. This pleased me, and I pretended that I was never happy unless it was on my knees. I kept it there for hours, stroking it so tender-ly, smoothing its thick white coat, which was always in the most perfect order, talking to it, caressing it.

And sometimes I took its head between my two hands, turned its face to mine, and stared into its large blue eyes. Then I could read all its agony, all its torture of apprehen-sion : and in spite of my friend's letters, and the dulness of my days, I was almost happy.

The summer was deepening, the glow of the roses flushed the garden ways, the skies were clear above Scawfell, when the end at last drew near. My grandmother's face was now scarcely recognizable. The eyes were sunk deep in her head. All expression seemed to fade gradually away. Her cheeks were no longer fine ivory white; a dull, sick-ening, yellow pallor overspread them. She seldom looked at me now, but rested en-tombed in her great armchair, her shrunken limbs seeming to tend downwards, as if she were inclined to slide to the floor and die there. Her lips were thin and dry, and moved perpetually in a silent chattering, as if her mind were talking and her voice were

already dead. The tide of life was retreating
from her body. I could almost see it visibly
ebb away. The failing waves made no sound
upon the shore. Death is uncanny, like all
silent things.

Her maid wished her to stay entirely in
bed, but she would get up, muttering that she
was well; and the doctor said it was useless
to hinder her. She had no specific disease.
Only the years were taking their last toll of
her. So she was placed in her chair each day
by the fire, and sat there till evening, muttering with those dry lips. The stiff folds of her
silken skirts formed an angle, and there the
cat crouched hour after hour, a silent, white,
waiting thing.

And the waves ebbed and ebbed away, and
I waited too.

One afternoon, as I sat by my grandmother, the servant entered with a letter for
me just arrived by the post. I took it up. It
was from Willoughby, my school-friend. He
said the term was over, that he had left
school, and his father had decided to send
him out to America to start in business in
New York, instead of entering him at Oxford
as he had hoped. He bade me good-bye, and
said he supposed we should not meet again
for years; "but," he added, "no doubt you

won't care a straw, so long as you get the confounded money you're after. You've taught me one of the lessons of life, young Ronald—never to believe in friendship."

As I read the letter I set my teeth. All that was good in my nature centred round Willoughby. He was a really fine fellow. I honestly and truly loved him. His news gave me a bitter shock, and turned my heart to iron and to fire. Perhaps I should never see him again; even if I did, time would have changed him, seared him—my friend, in his wonderful youth, with the morning in his eyes, would be no more. I hated myself in that moment for having stayed; I hated still more her who had kept me. For the moment I was carried out of myself. I crushed the letter up in my burning hand. I turned fiercely round upon that yellow, enigmatic, dying figure in the great chair. All the fury, locked within my heart for so long, rose to the surface, and drove self-interest away. I turned upon my grandmother with blazing eyes and trembling limbs. I opened my mouth to utter a torrent of reproachful words, when—what was it?—what slight change had stolen into the wrinkled, yellow face? I bent over her. The eyes gazed at me, but so horribly! She sat so low in her chair; she looked so fearful, so very strange. I put my fingers on her eyelids; I drew them down over the eyeballs: they did not open again. I felt her withered hands: they were ice. Then I knew, and I felt myself smiling. I leaned over the dead woman. There, on the far side of her, crouched the cat. Its white fur was all bristling; its blue eyes were dilated; on its jaws there were flecks of foam.

I leaned over the dead woman and took it in my arms.

.   .   .   .   .   .

That was nearly twenty years ago, and yet to-night the memory of that moment, and what followed it, bring a fear to my heart which I must combat. I have read of men who lived for long spaces of time haunted by demons created by their imagination, and I have laughed at them and pitied them. Surely I am not going to join in their folly, in their madness, led to the gates of terror by my own fancies, half-confirmed, apparently, by the chance utterances of a conceited Professor—a man of fads, although a man of science.

That was twenty years ago. After to-night let me forget it. After to-night, do I say? Hark! the birds are twittering in the dew outside.   The pale, early sun-shafts strike over the moors.   And I am tired.   To-morrow night I will finish this wrestle with my own folly; I will give the *coup de grâce* to my imagination.   But no more now.   My brain is not calm, and I will not write in excitement.

II.

WEDNESDAY NIGHT, *November 4th..*

MARGOT has gone to bed at last, and I am alone.   This has been a horrible day— horrible; but I will not dwell upon it.

After the death of my grandmother, I went back to school again.   But Willoughby was gone, and he could not forgive me.   He wrote to me once or twice from New York, and then I ceased to hear from him.   He died out of my life.   His affection for me had evidently declined from the day when he took it into his head that I was only a money-grubber, like the rest of the world, and that the Jew instinct had developed in me at an abnormally early age.   I let him go.   What did it matter?   But I was always glad that I had been cruel on the day my grandmother died.   I never repented of what I did—never. If I had, I might be happier now.

I went back to school.   I studied, played,

got into mischief and out of it again, like
other boys; but in my life there seemed to
be an eternal coldness, that I alone, perhaps,
was conscious of. My deed of cruelty, of
brutal revenge on the thing that had never
done me injury, had seared my soul. I was
not sorry, but I could not forget; and sometimes I thought—how ridiculous it looks
written down!—that there was a power hidden somewhere which could not forget either,
and that a penalty might have to be paid.
Because a creature is dumb, must its soul die
when it dies? Is not the soul, perhaps—as
he said—a wanderer through many bodies?

But if I did not kill a soul, as I killed a
body, the day my grandmother died, where is
that soul now? That is what I want to arrive at, that is what I must arrive at, if I am
to be happy.

I went back to school, and I passed to
Oxford. I tasted the strange, unique life of
a university, narrow, yet pulsating, where the
youth, that is so green and springing, tries to
arm itself for the battle with the weapons
forged by the dead and sharpened by the
more elderly among the living. I did well
there, and I passed on into the world. And
then at last I began to understand the value
of my inheritance; for all that had been my

grandmother's was now mine. My people wished me to marry, but I had no desire to fetter myself. So I took the sponge in my strong young hands, and tried to squeeze it dry. And I did not know that I was sad—I did not know it until, at the age of thirty-three, just seventeen years after my grandmother died, I understood the sort of thing happiness is. Of course, it was love that brought to me understanding. I need not explain that. I had often played on love; now love began to play on me. I trembled at the harmonies his hands evoked.

I met a young girl, very young, just on the verge of life and of womanhood. She was seventeen when I first saw her, and she was valsing at a big ball in London—her first ball. She passed me in the crowd of dancers, and I noticed her. As she was a *débutante* her dress was naturally snow-white. There was no touch of colour about it—not a flower, not a jewel. Her hair was the palest yellow I had almost ever seen—the colour of an early primrose. Naturally fluffy, it nearly concealed the white riband that ran through it, and clustered in tendrils and tiny natural curls upon her neck. Her skin was whiter than ivory—a clear, luminous white. Her eyes were very large and china-blue in colour.

This young girl dancing passed and re-
passed me, and my glance rested on her idly,
even cynically.　For she seemed so happy,
and at that time happiness won my languid
wonder, if ingenuously exhibited.　To be
happy seemed almost to be mindless.　But
by degrees I found myself watching this girl,
and more closely.　Another dance began.　She
joined it with another partner.　But she seemed
just as pleased with him as with her former
one.　She would not let him pause to rest;
she kept him dancing all the time, her youth
and freshness spoken in that gentle compel-
ling.　I grew interested in her, even acutely
so.　She seemed to me like the spirit of youth
dancing over the body of Time.　I resolved
to know her.　I felt weary; I thought she
might revive me.　The dance drew to an end,
and I approached my hostess, pointed the
girl out, and asked for an introduction.　Her
name was Margot Magendie, I found, and she
was an heiress as well as a beauty.

I did not care.　It was her humanity that
drew me, nothing else.

But, strange to say, when the moment for
the introduction arrived, and I stood face to
face with Miss Magendie, I felt an extraordinary shrinking from her.　I have never been
able to understand it, but my blood ran cold,

and my pulses almost ceased to beat. I would have avoided her; an instinct within me seemed suddenly to cry out against her. But it was too late : the introduction was effected; her hand rested on my arm.

I was actually trembling. She did not appear to notice it. The band played a valse, and the inexplicable horror that had seized me lost itself in the gay music. It never returned until lately.

I seldom enjoyed a valse more. Our steps suited so perfectly, and her obvious childish pleasure communicated itself to me. The spirit of youth in her knocked on my rather jaded heart, and I opened to it. That was beautiful and strange. I talked with her, and I felt myself younger, ingenuous rather than cynical, inclined even to a radiant, though foolish, optimism. She was very natural, very imperfect in worldly education, full of fragmentary but decisive views on life, quite unabashed in giving them forth, quite inconsiderate in summoning my adherence to them.

And then, presently, as we sat in a dim corridor under a rosy hanging lamp, in saying something she looked, with her great blue eyes, right into my face. Some very faint recollection awoke and stirred in my mind.

"Surely," I said hesitatingly—"surely I
have seen you before? It seems to me that
I remember your eyes."

As I spoke I was thinking hard, chasing
the vagrant recollection that eluded me.

She smiled.

"You don't remember my face?"

"No, not at all."

"Nor I yours. If we had seen each other,
surely we should recollect it."

Then she blushed, suddenly realizing that
her words implied, perhaps, more than she
had meant. I did not pay the obvious compliment. Those blue eyes and something in
their expression moved me strangely; but I
could not tell why. When I said good-bye
to her that night, I asked to be allowed to
call.

She assented.

That was the beginning of a very beautiful courtship, which gave a colour to life, a
music to existence, a meaning to every slightest sensation.

And was it love that laid to sleep recollection, that sang a lullaby to awakening horror, and strewed poppies over it till it sighed
itself into slumber? Was it love that drowned
my mind in deep and charmed waters, binding the strange powers that every mind pos-

sesses in flowery garlands stronger than any
fetters of iron? Was it love that, calling up
dreams, alienated my thoughts from their
search after reality?

I hardly know. I only know that I grew
to love Margot, and only looked for love in
her blue eyes, not for any deed of the past
that might be mirrored there.

And I made her love me.

She gave her child's heart to my keeping
with a perfect confidence that only a perfect
affection could engender. She did love me
then. No circumstances of to-day can break
that fact under their hammers. She did love
me, and it is the knowledge that she did
which gives so much of fear to me now.

For great changes in the human mind are
terrible. As we realize them we realize the
limitless possibilities of sinister deeds that lie
hidden in every human being. A little child
that loves a doll can become an old, crafty,
secret murderer. How horrible!

And perhaps it is still more horrible to
think that, while the human envelope remains
totally unchanged, every word of the letter
within may become altered, and a message of
peace fade into a sentence of death.

Margot's face is the same face now as it
was when I married her—scarcely older, cer-

tainly not less beautiful. Only the expression of the eyes has changed.

For we were married. After a year of love-making, which never tired either of us, we elected to bind ourselves, to fuse the two into one.

We went abroad for the honeymoon, and, instead of shortening it to the fashionable fortnight, we travelled for nearly six months, and were happy all the time.

Boredom never set in. Margot had a beautiful mind as well as a beautiful face. She softened me through my affection. The current of my life began to set in a different direction. I turned the pages of a book of pity and of death more beautiful than that of Pierre Loti. I could hear at last the great cry for sympathy, which is the music of this strange suffering world, and, listening to it, in my heart there rang an echo. The cruelty in my nature seemed to shrivel up. I was more gentle than I had been, more gentle than I had thought I could ever be.

At last, in the late spring, we started for home. We stayed for a week in London, and then we travelled north. Margot had never seen her future home, had never even been in Cumberland before. She was full of excitement and happiness, a veritable child in the

6

ready and ardent expression of her feelings. The station is several miles from the house, and is on the edge of the sea. When the train pulled up at the wayside platform the day drew towards sunset, and the flat levels of the beach shone with a rich, liquid, amber light. In the distance the sea was tossing and tumbling, whipped into foam by a fresh wind. The Isle of Man lay far away, dark, mysterious, under a stack of bellying white clouds, just beginning to be tinged with the faintest rose.

Margot found the scene beautiful, the wind life-giving, the flat sand-banks, the shining levels, even.the dry, spiky grass that fluttered in the breeze, fascinating and re-freshing.

"I feel near the heart of Nature in a place like this," she said, looking up at a sea-gull that hovered over the little platform, crying to the wind on which it hung.

The train stole off along the edge of the sands, till we could see only the white stream-er of its smoke trailing towards the sun. We turned away from the sea, got into the car-riage that was waiting for us, and set our faces inland. The ocean was blotted out by the low grass and heather-covered banks that divided the fields. Presently we plunged into woods. The road descended sharply. A village, an abruptly winding river sprang into sight.

We were on my land. We passed the inn, the Rainwood Arms, named after my grandfather's family. The people whom we met stared curiously and saluted in rustic fashion.

Margot was full of excitement and pleasure, and talked incessantly, holding my hand tightly in hers and asking a thousand questions. Passing through the village, we mounted a hill towards a thick grove of trees.

"The house stands among them," I said, pointing.

She sprang up eagerly in the carriage to find it, but it was hidden.

We dashed through the gate into the momentary darkness of the drive, emerged between great green lawns, and drew up before the big doorway of the hall. I looked into her eyes, and said "Welcome!"

She only smiled in answer.

I would not let her enter the house immediately, but made her come with me to the terrace above the river, to see the view over the Cumbrian mountains and the moors of Eskdale.

The sky was very clear and pale, but over Styhead the clouds were boiling up. The

Screes that guard ebon Wastwater looked grim and sad.

Margot stood beside me on the terrace, but her chatter had been succeeded by silence. And I, too, was silent for the moment, absorbed in contemplation. But presently I turned to her, wishing to see how she was impressed by her new domain.

She was not looking towards the river and the hills, but at the terrace walk itself, the band of emerald turf that bordered it, the stone pots full of flowers, the winding way that led into the shrubbery.

She was looking at these intently, and with a strangely puzzled, almost startled expression.

"Hush! Don't speak to me for a moment," she said, as I opened my lips. "Don't; I want to—— How odd this is!"

And she gazed up at the windows of the house, at the creepers that climbed its walls, at the sloping roof and the irregular chimney-stacks.

Her lips were slightly parted, and her eyes were full of an inward expression that told me she was struggling with forgetfulness and desired recollection.

I was silent, wondering.

At last she said: "Ronald, I have never

been in the North of England before, never set foot in Cumberland; yet I seem to know this terrace walk, those very flower-pots, the garden, the look of that roof, those chimneys, even the slanting way in which that great creeper climbs. Is it not—is it not very strange?"

She gazed up at me, and in her blue eyes there was an expression almost of fear.

I smiled down on her. "It must be your fancy," I said.

"It does not seem so," she replied. "I feel as if I had been here before, and often, or for a long time." She paused; then she said: "Do let me go into the house. There ought to be a room there—a room—I seem almost to see it. Come! Let us go in."

She took my hand and drew me towards the hall door. The servants were carrying in the luggage, and there was a certain amount of confusion and noise, but she did not seem to notice it. She was intent on something; I could not tell what.

"Do show me the house, Ronald—the drawing-room, and—and—there is another room I wish to see."

"You shall see them all, dear," I said. "You are excited. It is natural enough. This is the drawing-room."

She glanced round it hastily.

"And now the others!" she exclaimed.

I took her to the dining-room, the library, and the various apartments on the ground-floor.

She scarcely looked at them. When we had finished exploring, "Are these all?" she asked, with a wavering accent of disappointment.

"All," I answered.

"Then—show me the rooms upstairs."

We ascended the shallow oak steps, and passed first into the apartment in which my grandmother had died.

It had been done up since then, refurnished, and almost completely altered. Only the wide fireplace, with its brass dogs and its heavy oaken mantelpiece, had been left untouched.

Margot glanced hastily round. Then she walked up to the fireplace, and drew a long breath.

"There ought to be a fire here," she said.

"But it is summer," I answered, wondering.

"And a chair there," she went on, in a curious low voice, indicating—I think now, or is it my imagination?—the very spot where my grandmother was wont to sit. "Yes—I seem to remember, and yet not to remember."

She looked at me, and her white brows were knit.

Suddenly she said: "Ronald, I don't think I like this room. There is something—I don't know—I don't think I could sit here; and I seem to remember—something about it, as I did about the terrace. What can it mean?"

"It means that you are tired and over-excited, darling. Your nerves are too highly strung, and nerves play us strange tricks. Come to your own room and take off your things, and when you have had some tea, you will be all right again."

Yes, I was fool enough to believe that tea was the panacea for an undreamed-of, a then unimaginable, evil.

I thought Margot was simply an overtired and imaginative child that evening. If I could believe so now!

We went up into her boudoir and had tea, and she grew more like herself; but several times that night I observed her looking puzzled and thoughtful, and a certain expression of anxiety shone in her blue eyes that was new to them then.

But I thought nothing of it, and I was-
happy. Two or three days passed, and Margot did not again refer to her curious sensation of pre-knowledge of the house and garden. I fancied there was a slight alteration
in her manner; that was all. She seemed a
little restless. Her vivacity flagged now and
then. She was more willing to be alone than
she had been. But we were old married folk
now, and could not be always in each other's
sight. I had a great many people connected
with the estate to see, and had to gather up
the tangled threads of many affairs.

The honeymoon was over. Of course we
could not always be together.

Still, I should have wished Margot to desire it, and I could not hide from myself that
now and then she scarcely concealed a slight
impatience to be left in solitude. This troubled me, but only a little, for she was generally as fond as ever. That evening, however,
an incident occurred which rendered me decidedly uneasy, and made me wonder if my
wife were not inclined to that curse of highly-
strung women—hysteria!

I had been riding over the moors to visit
a tenant-farmer who lived at some distance,
and did not return until twilight. Dismount-
ing, I let myself into the house, traversed the

hall, and ascended the stairs. As I wore
spurs, and the steps were of polished oak and
uncarpeted, I walked noisily enough to warn
anyone of my approach. I was passing the
door of the room that had been my grandmother's sitting-room, when I noticed that it
stood open. The house was rather dark, and
the interior was dim enough, but I could see
a figure in a white dress moving about inside.
I recognised Margot, and wondered what she
was doing, but her movements were so singu-
lar that, instead of speaking to her, I stood
in the doorway and watched her.

She was walking, with a very peculiar,
stealthy step, around the room, not as if she
were looking for anything, but merely as if
she were restless or ill at ease. But what
struck me forcibly was this, that there was
something curiously animal in her movements, seen thus in a dim half-light that only
partially revealed her to me. I had never
seen a woman walk in that strangely wild yet
soft way before. There was something uncanny about it, that rendered me extremely
discomforted; yet I was quite fascinated, and
rooted to the ground.

I cannot tell how long I stood there. I
was so completely absorbed in the passion of
the gazer that the passage of time did not

concern me in the least. I was as one assisting at a strange spectacle. This white thing moving in the dark did not suggest my wife to me, although it was she. I might have been watching an animal, vague, yet purposeful of mind, tracing out some hidden thing, following out some instinct quite foreign to humanity. I remember that presently I involuntarily clasped my hands together, and felt that they were very cold. Perspiration broke out on my face. I was painfully, unnaturally moved, and a violent desire to be away from this white moving thing came over me. Walking as softly as I could, I went to my dressing-room, shut the door, and sat down on a chair. I never remember to have felt thoroughly unnerved before, but now I found myself actually shaken, palsied. I could understand how deadly a thing fear is. I lit a candle hastily, and as I did so a knock came to the door.

Margot's voice said, " May I come in ? "

I felt unable to reply, so I got up and admitted her.   .

She entered smiling, and looking such a child, so innocent, so tender, that I almost laughed aloud. That I, a man, should have been frightened by a child in a white dress, just because the twilight cast a phantom at-

mosphere around her! I held her in my
arms, and I gazed into her blue eyes.

She looked down, but still smiled.

"Where have you been, and what have
you been doing?" I asked gaily.

She answered that she had been in the
drawing-room since tea-time.

"You came here straight from the drawing-room?" I said.

She replied, "Yes.",

Then, with an indifferent air which hid
real anxiety, I said:

"By the way, Margot, have you been into
that room again—the room you fancied, you
recollected?"

"No, never," she answered, withdrawing
herself from my arms. "I don't wish to go
there. Make haste, Ronald, and dress. It
is nearly dinner-time, and I am ready." And
she turned and left me.

She had told me a lie. All my feelings
of uneasiness and discomfort returned ten-
fold.

That evening was the most wretched one,
the only wretched one, I had ever spent with
her.

.   .   .   .   .   .

I am tired of writing. I will continue my
task to-morrow. It takes me longer than I

anticipated. Yet even to tell everything to myself brings me some comfort. Man must express himself; and despair must find a voice.

III.

THURSDAY NIGHT, *December 5th.*

THAT lie awoke in me suspicion of the child I had married. I began to doubt her, yet never ceased to love her. She had all my heart, and must have it till the end. But the calm of love was to be succeeded by love's tumult and agony. A strangeness was creeping over Margot. It was as if she took a thin veil in her hands, and drew it over and all around her, till the outlines I had known were slightly blurred. Her disposition, which had been so clear cut, so sharply, beautifully defined, standing out in its innocent glory for all men to see, seemed to withdraw itself, as if a dawning necessity for secrecy had arisen. A thin crust of reserve began to subtly overspread her every act and expression. She thought now before she spoke; she thought before she looked. It seemed to me that she was becoming a slightly different person.

The change I mean to imply is very difficult to describe. It was not abrupt enough to startle, but I could feel it, slight though it

was. Have you seen the first flat film of
waveless water, sent by the incoming tides
of the sea, crawling silently up over the
wrinkled brown sand, and filling the tiny
ruts, till diminutive hills and valleys are all
one smooth surface ? So it was with Margot.
A tide flowed over her character, a waveless
tide of reserve. The hills and valleys which
I loved disappeared from my ken. Behind
the old sweet smile, the old frank expression,
my wife was shrinking down to hide herself,
as one escaping from pursuit hides behind a
barrier. When one human being knows another very intimately, and all the barricades
that divide soul from soul have been broken
down, it is difficult to set them up again without noise and dust, and the sound of thrust-
in bolts, and the tap of the hammer that
drives in the nails. It is difficult, but not impossible. Barricades can be raised noiseless-
ly, soundless bolts—that keep out the soul—
be pushed home. The black gauze veil that
blots out the scene drops, and when it is
raised—if ever—the scene is changed.

The real Margot was receding from me.
I felt it with an impotence of despair that was
benumbing. Yet I could not speak of it, for
at first I could hardly tell if she knew of what
was taking place. Indeed, at this moment,

in thinking it over, I do not believe that for some time she had any definite cognisance of the fact that she was growing to love me less passionately than of old. In acts she was not changed. That was the strange part of the matter. Her kisses were warm, but I believed them premeditated. She clasped my hand in hers, but now there was more mechanism than magic in that act of tenderness. Impulse failed within her ; and she had been all impulse ? Did she know it ? At that time I wondered. Believing that she did not know she was changing, I was at the greatest pains to guard my conduct, lest I should implant the suspicion that might hasten what I feared. I remained, desperately, the same as ever, and so, of course, was not the same, for a deed done defiantly bears little resemblance to a deed done naturally. I was always considering what I should say, how I should act, even how I should look. To live now was sedulous instead of easy. Effort took the place of simplicity. My wife and I were gazing furtively at each other through the eye-holes of masks. I knew it. Did she ?

At that time I never ceased to wonder. Of one thing I was certain, however—that Margot began to devise excuses for being left alone. When we first came home she

could hardly endure me out of her sight.
Now she grew to appreciate solitude. This
was a terrible danger signal, and I could not
fail to so regard it.

Yet something within me held me back
from speaking out. I made no comment on
the change that deepened day by day, but I
watched my wife furtively, with a concentra-
tion of attention that sometimes left me physically exhausted. I felt, too, at length, that
I was growing morbid, that suspicion coloured
my mind and caused me, perhaps, to put a
wrong interpretation on many of her actions,
to exaggerate and misconstrue the most simple things she did. I began to believe her
every look premeditated. Even if she kissed
me, I thought she did it with a purpose; if
she smiled up at me as of old, I fancied the
smile to be only a concealment of its opposite. By degrees we became shy of each
other. We were like uncongenial intimates,
forced to occupy the same house, forced into
a fearful knowledge of each other's personal
habits, while we knew nothing of the thoughts
that make up the true lives of individuals.

And then another incident occurred, a
pendant to the incident of Margot's strange
denied visit to the room she affected to fear.
It was one night, one deep dark night of the

autumn—a season to affect even a cheerful mind and incline it towards melancholy. Margot and I were now often silent when we were together. That evening, towards nine, a dull steady rain set in. I remember I heard it on the window-panes as we sat in the drawing-room after dinner, and remarked on it, saying to her that if it continued for two or three days she might chance to see the floods out, and that fishermen would descend upon us by the score.

I did not obtain much response from her. The dreariness of the weather seemed to affect her spirits. She took up a book presently, and appeared to read; but, once in glancing up suddenly from my newspaper, I thought I caught her gaze fixed fearfully upon me. It seemed to me that she was looking furtively at me with an absolute terror. I was so much affected that I made some excuse for leaving the room, went down to my den, lit a cigar, and walked uneasily up and down, listening to the rain on the window. At ten Margot came in to tell me she was going to bed. I wished her good-night tenderly, but as I held her slim body a moment in my arms I felt that she began to tremble. I let her go, and she slipped from the room with the soft, cushioned step that

was habitual with her. And, strangely enough,
my thoughts recurred to the day, long ago,
when I first held the great white cat on my
knees, and felt its body shrink from my touch
with a nameless horror. The uneasy movement of the woman recalled to me so strongly and so strangely the uneasy movement of
the animal.

I lit a second cigar. It was near midnight
when it was smoked out, and I turned down
the lamp and went softly up to bed. I un-
dressed in the room adjoining my wife's, and
then stole into hers. She was sleeping in the
wide white bed rather uneasily, and as I
leaned over her, shading the candle flame
with my outspread hand, she muttered some
broken words that I could not catch. I had
never heard her talk in her dreams before. I
lay down gently at her side and extinguished
the candle.

But sleep did not come to me. The dull,
dead silence weighed upon instead of soothing me. My mind was terribly alive, in a
ferment; and the contrast between my own
excitement and the hushed peace of my environment was painful, was almost unbeara-
ble. I wished that a wind from the mountains
were beating against the window-panes, and
the rain lashing the house in fury. The black

7

calm around was horrible, unnatural. The
drizzling rain was now so small that I could
not even hear its patter when I strained my
ears. Margot had ceased to mutter, and lay
perfectly still. How I longed to be able to
read the soul hidden in her sleeping body, to
unravel the mystery of the mind which I had
once understood so perfectly! It is so horrible that we can never open the human envelope, take out the letter, and seize with our
eyes upon its every word. Margot slept with
all her secrets safeguarded, although she was
unconscious, no longer watchful, on the alert.
She was so silent, even her quiet breathing
not reaching my ear, that I felt impelled to
stretch out my hand beneath the coverlet and
touch hers ever so softly. I did so.

Her hand was instantly and silently withdrawn. She was awake, then.

" Margot," I said, " did I disturb you ? "

There was no answer.

The movement, followed by the silence,
affected me very disagreeably.

I lit the candle and looked at her. She
was lying on the extreme edge of the bed,
with her blue eyes closed. Her lips were
slightly parted. I could hear her steady
breathing. Yet was she really sleeping ?

I bent lower over her, and as I did so a

slight, involuntary movement, akin to what we call a shudder, ran through her body. I recoiled from the bed. An impotent anger seized me. Could it be that my presence was becoming so hateful to my wife that even in sleep her body trembled when I drew near it? Or was this slumber feigned? I could not tell, but I felt it impossible at that moment to remain in the room. I returned to my own, dressed, and descended the stairs to the door opening on to the terrace. I felt a longing to be out in the air. The atmosphere of the house was stifling.

Was it coming to this, then? Did I, a man, shrink with a fantastic cowardice from a woman I loved? The latent cruelty began to stir within me, the tyrant spirit which a strong love sometimes evokes. I had been Margot's slave almost. My affection had brought me to her feet, had kept me there. So long as she loved me I was content to be her captive, knowing she was mine. But a change in her attitude toward me might rouse the master. In my nature there was a certain brutality, a savagery, which I had never wholly slain, although Margot had softened me wonderfully by her softness, had brought me to gentleness by her tenderness. The boy of years ago had developed toward better things, but he was not dead in me. I felt that as I walked up and down the terrace through the night in a wild meditation. If my love could not hold Margot, my strength should.

I drew in a long breath of the wet night air, and I opened my shoulders as if shaking off an oppression. My passion for Margot had not yet drawn me down to weakness; it had raised me up to strength. The faint fear of her, which I had felt almost without knowing it more than once, died within me. The desire of the conqueror elevated me. There was something for me to win. My paralysis passed away, and I turned toward the house.

And now a strange thing happened. I walked into the dark hall, closed the outer door, shutting out the dull murmur of the night, and felt in my pocket for my match-box. It was not there. I must inadvertently have laid it down in my dressing-room and left it. I searched about in the darkness on the hall table, but could find no light. There was nothing for it, then, but to feel my way upstairs as best I could.

I started, keeping my hand against the wall to guide me. I gained the top of the stairs, and began to traverse the landing, still with my hand upon the wall. To reach my dressing-room I had to pass the apartment which had been my grandmother's sitting-room.

When I reached it, instead of sliding along a closed door, as I had anticipated, my hand dropped into vacancy.

The door was wide open. It had been shut, like all the other doors in the house, when I had descended the stairs—shut and locked, as it always was at night-time. Why was it open now?

I paused in the darkness. And then an impulse seized me to walk forward into the room. I advanced a step; but, as I did so, a horrible low cry broke upon my ears out of the darkness. It came from immediately in front of me, and sounded like an expression of the most abject fear.

My feet rooted themselves to the ground.

"Who's there?" I asked.

There came no answer.

I listened for a moment, but did not hear the minutest sound. The desire for light was overpowering. I generally did my writing in this room, and knew the exact whereabouts of everything in it. I knew that on the writing-table there was a silver box containing wax matches. It lay on the left of my desk. I moved another step forward.

There was the sound of a slight rustle, as if someone shrank back as I advanced.

I laid my hand quickly on the box, opened it, and struck a light. The room was vaguely illuminated. I saw something white at the far end, against the wall. I put the match to a candle.

The white thing was Margot. She was in her dressing-gown, and was crouched up in an angle of the wall as far away from where I stood as possible. Her blue eyes were wide open, and fixed upon me with an expression of such intense and hideous fear in them that I almost cried out.

"Margot, what is the matter?" I said. "Are you ill?"

She made no reply. Her face terrified me.

"What is it, Margot?" I cried in a loud, almost harsh voice, determined to rouse her from this horrible, unnatural silence. "What are you doing here?"

I moved towards her. I stretched out my hands and seized her. As I did so, a sort of sob burst from her. Her hands were cold and trembling.

"What is it? What has frightened you?" I reiterated.

At last she spoke in a low voice.

"You—you looked so strange, so—so cruel as you came in," she said.

"Strange! Cruel! But you could not see me. It was dark," I answered.

"Dark!" she said.

"Yes, until I lit the candle. And you cried out when I was only in the doorway. You could not see me there."

"Why not? What has that got to do with it?" she murmured, still trembling violently.

"You can see me in the dark?"

"Of course," she said. "I don't understand what you mean. Of course I can see you when you are there before my eyes."

"But——" I began; and then her obvious and complete surprise at my questions stopped them. I still held her hands in mine, and their extreme coldness roused me to the remembrance that she was unclothed.

"You will be ill if you stay here," I said. "Come back to your room."

She said nothing, and I led her back, waited while she got into bed, and then, placing the candle on the dressing-table, sat down in a chair by her side.

The strong determination to take prompt action, to come to an explanation, to end these dreary mysteries of mind and conduct, was still upon me.

I did not think of the strange hour; I did not care that the night was gliding on towards dawn. I was self-absorbed. I was beyond ordinary considerations.

Yet I did not speak immediately. I was trying to be quite calm, trying to think of the best line for me to take. So much might depend upon our mere words now. At length I said, laying my hand upon hers, which was outside the coverlet:

"Margot, what were you doing in that room at such a strange hour? Why were you there?"

She hesitated obviously. Then she answered, not looking at me:

"I missed you. I thought you might be there—writing."

"But you were in the dark."

"I thought you would have a light."

I knew by her manner that she was not telling me the truth, but I went on quietly:

"If you expected me, why did you cry out when I came to the door?"

She tried to draw her hand away, but I held it fast, closing my fingers upon it with even brutal strength.

"Why did you cry out?"

"You—you looked so strange, so cruel."

"So cruel!"

"Yes. You frightened me—you frightened me horribly."

She began suddenly to sob, like one completely overstrained. I lifted her up in the bed, put my arms round her, and made her lean against me. I was strangely moved.

"I frightened you! How can that be?" I said, trying to control a passion of mingled love and anger that filled my breast. "You know that I love you. You must know that. In all our short married life have I ever been even momentarily unkind to you? Let us be frank with one another. Our lives have changed lately. One of us has altered. You cannot say that it is I."

She only continued to sob bitterly in my arms. I held her closer.

"Let us be frank with one another," I went on. "For God's sake let us have no barriers between us. Margot, look into my eyes and tell me—are you growing tired of me?"

She turned her head away, but I spoke more sternly:

"You shall be truthful. I will have no more subterfuge. Look me in the face. You did love me once?"

"Yes, yes," she whispered in a choked voice.

"What have I done, then, to alienate you? Have I ever hurt you, ever shown a lack of sympathy, ever neglected you?"

"Never—never."

"Yet you have changed to me since—since——" I paused a moment, trying to recall when I had first noticed her altered demeanour.

She interrupted me.

"It has all come upon me in this house," she sobbed. "Oh! what is it? What does it all mean? If I could understand a little—only a little—it would not be so bad. But this nightmare, this thing that seems such a madness of the intellect——"

Her voice broke and ceased. Her tears burst forth afresh. Such mingled fear, passion, and a sort of strange latent irritation, I had never seen before.

"It is a madness indeed," I said, and a sense almost of outrage made my voice hard and cold. "I have not deserved such treatment at your hands."

"I will not yield to it," she said, with a sort of desperation, suddenly throwing her arms around me. "I will not—I will not!"

I was strangely puzzled. I was torn with

conflicting feelings. Love and anger grappled at my heart. But I only held her, and did not speak until she grew obviously calmer. The paroxysm seemed passing away. Then I said :

"I cannot understand."

"Nor I," she answered, with a directness that had been foreign to her of late, but that was part and parcel of her real, beautiful nature. "I cannot understand. I only know there is a change in me, or in you to me, and that I cannot help it, or that I have not been able to help it. Sometimes I feel— do not be angry, I will try to tell you—a physical fear of you, of your touch, of your clasp, a fear such as an animal might feel towards the master who had beaten it. I tremble then at your approach. When you are near me I feel cold, oh! so cold and— and anxious ; perhaps I ought to say apprehensive. Oh, I am hurting you!"

I suppose I must have winced at her words, and she is quick to observe.

"Go on," I said ; "do not spare me. Tell me everything. It is madness indeed ; but we may kill it, when we both know it."

"Oh, if we could!" she cried, with a poignancy which was heart-breaking to hear. "If we could!"

"Do you doubt our ability?" I said, trying to be patient and calm. "You are unreasoning, like all women. Be sensible for a moment. You do me a wrong in cherishing these feelings. I have the capacity for cruelty in me. I may have been—I have been —cruel in the past, but never to you. You have no right to treat me as you have done lately. If you examine your feelings, and compare them with facts, you will see their absurdity."

"But," she interposed, with a woman's fatal quickness, "that will not do away with their reality."

"It must. Look into their faces until they fade like ghosts, seen only between light and darkness. They are founded upon nothing; they are bred without father or mother; they are hysterical; they are wicked. Think a little of me. You are not going to be conquered by a chimera, to allow a phantom created by your imagination to ruin the happiness that has been so beautiful. You will not do that! You dare not!"

She only answered:

"If I can help it."

A passionate anger seized me, a fury at my impotence against this child. I pushed her almost roughly from my arms.

"And I have married this woman!" I cried bitterly. I got up.

Margot had ceased crying now, and her face was very white and calm; it looked rigid in the faint candle-light that shone across the bed.

"Do not be angry," she said. "We are controlled by something inside of us; there are powers in us that we cannot fight against."

"There is nothing we cannot fight against," I said passionately. "The doctrine of predestination is the devil's own doctrine. It is the doctrine set up by the sinner to excuse his sin; it is the coward's doctrine. Understand me, Margot, I love you, but I am not a weak fool. There must be an end of this folly. Perhaps you are playing with me, acting like a girl, testing me. Let us have no more of it."

She said:

"I only do what I must."

Her tone turned me cold. Her set face frightened me, and angered me, for there was a curious obstinacy in it. I left the room abruptly, and did not return. That night I had no sleep.

I am not a coward, but I find that I am inclined to fear that which fears me. I dread

an animal that always avoids me silently
more than an animal that actually attacks
me. The thing that runs from me makes me
shiver, the thing that creeps away when I
come near wakes my uneasiness. At this
time there rose up in me a strange feeling
towards Margot. The white, fair child I had
married was at moments—only at moments—
horrible to me. I felt disposed to shun her.
Something within cried out against her.
Long ago, at the instant of our introduction,
an unreasoning sensation that could only be
called dread had laid hold upon me. That
dread returned from the night of our explanation, returned deepened and added to. It
prompted me to a suggestion which I had no
sooner made than I regretted it. On the
morning following I told Margot that in future we had better occupy separate rooms.
She assented quietly, but I thought a furtive
expression of relief stole for a moment into
her face.

I was deeply angered with her and with
myself; yet, now that I knew beyond question my wife's physical terror of me, I was
half afraid of her. I felt as if I could not
bring myself to lie long hours by her side in
the darkness, by the side of a woman who
was shrinking from me, who was watching

me when I could not see her.   The idea made
my very flesh creep.

Yet I hated myself for this shrinking of
the body, and sometimes hated her for rous-
ing it.   A hideous struggle was going on
within me—a struggle between love and impotent anger and despair, between the lover
and the master.   For I am one of the old-
fashioned men who think that a husband ought
to be master of his wife as well as of his house.

How could I be master of a woman I secretly feared?   My knowledge of myself
spurred me through acute irritation almost
to the verge of madness.

All calm was gone.   I was alternately
gentle to my wife and almost ferocious
towards her, ready to fall at her feet and
worship her or to seize her and treat her with
physical violence.   I only restrained myself
by an effort.

My variations of manner did not seem to
affect her.   Indeed, it sometimes struck me
that she feared me more when I was kind to
her than when I was harsh.

And I knew, by a thousand furtive indica-
tions, that her horror of me was deepening
day by day.   I believe she could hardly bring
herself to be in a room alone with me, especially after nightfall.

One evening, when we were dining, the butler, after placing dessert upon the table, moved to leave us. She turned white, and, as he reached the door, half rose, and called him back in a sharp voice.

"Symonds!" she said.

"Yes, ma'am?"

"You are going?"

The fellow looked surprised.

"Can I get you anything, ma'am?"

She glanced at me with an indescribable uneasiness. Then she leaned back in her chair with an effort, and pressed her lips together.

"No," she said.

As the man went out and shut the door, she looked at me again from under her eyelids; and finally her eyes travelled from me to a small, thin-bladed knife, used for cutting oranges, that lay near her plate, and fixed themselves on it. She put out her hand stealthily, drew it towards her, and kept her hand over it on the table. I took an orange from a dish in front of me.

"Margot," I said, "will you pass me that fruit-knife?"

She obviously hesitated.

"Give me that knife," I repeated roughly, stretching out my hand.

She lifted her hand, left the knife upon

the table, and at the same time, springing up, glided softly out of the room and closed the door behind her.

That evening I spent alone in the smoking-room, and, for the first time, she did not come to bid me good-night.

I sat smoking my cigar in a tumult of furious despair and love. The situation was becoming intolerable. It could not be endured. I longed for a crisis, even for a violent one. I could have cried aloud that night for a veritable tragedy. There were moments when I would almost have killed the child who mysteriously eluded and defied me. I could have wreaked a cruel vengeance upon the body for the sin of the mind. I was terribly, mortally distressed.

After a long and painful self-communion, I resolved to make another wild effort to set things right before it was too late; and when the clock chimed the half-hour after ten I went upstairs softly to her bedroom and turned the handle of the door, meaning to enter, to catch Margot in my arms, tell her how deep my love for her was, how she injured me by her base fears, and how she was driving me back from the gentleness she had given me to the cruelty, to the brutality, of my first nature.

8

The door resisted me: it was locked.

I paused a moment, and then tapped gently. I heard a sudden rustle within, as if someone hurried across the floor away from the door, and then Margot's voice cried sharply:

"Who's that? Who is there?"

"Margot, it is I. I wish to speak to you —to say good-night."

"Good-night," she said.

"But let me in for a moment."

There was a silence—it seemed to me a long one; then she answered:

"Not now, dear; I—I am so tired."

"Open the door for a moment."

"I am very tired. Good-night."

The cold, level tone of her voice—for the anxiety had left it after that first sudden cry—roused me to a sudden fury of action. I seized the handle of the door and pressed with all my strength. Physically I am a very powerful man—my anger and despair gave me a giant's might. I burst the lock, and sprang into the room. My impulse was to seize Margot in my arms and crush her to death, it might be, in an embrace she could not struggle against. The blood coursed like molten fire through my veins. The lust of love, the lust of murder even, perhaps, was upon me. I sprang impetuously into the room.

No candles were alight in it. The blinds were up, and the chill moonbeams filtered through the small lattice panes. By the farthest window, in the yellowish radiance, was huddled a white thing.

A sudden cold took hold upon me. All the warmth in me froze up.

I stopped where I was and held my breath.

That white thing, seen thus uncertainly, had no semblance to humanity. It was animal wholly. I could have believed for the moment that a white cat crouched from me there by the curtain, waiting to spring.

What a strange illusion that was! I tried to laugh at it afterwards, but at the moment horror stole through me—horror, and almost awe.

All desire of violence left me. Heat was dead; I felt cold as stone. I could not even speak a word.

Suddenly the white thing moved. The curtain was drawn sharply; the moonlight was blotted out; the room was plunged in darkness—a darkness in which that thing could see!

I turned and stole out of the room. I

could have fled, driven by the nameless fear
that was upon me.

Only when the morning dawned did the
man in me awake, and I cursed myself for
my cowardice.

   .   .   .   .   .   .

The following evening we were asked to
dine out with some neighbours, who lived a
few miles off in a wonderful old Norman
castle near the sea. During the day neither
of us had made the slightest allusion to the
incidents of the previous night. We both
felt it a relief to go into society, I think.
The friends to whom we went—Lord and
Lady Melchester—had a large party staying
with them, and we were, I believe, the only
outsiders who lived in the neighbourhood.
One of their guests was Professor Black,
whose name I have already mentioned—a
little, dry, thin, acrid man, with thick black
hair, innocent of the comb, and pursed,
straight lips. I had met him two or three
times in London, and as he had only just
arrived at the castle, and scarcely knew his
fellow-visitors there, he brought his wine
over to me when the ladies left the dining-
room, and entered into conversation. At the
moment I was glad, but before we followed
the women I would have given a year—I

might say years—of my life not to have spoken to him, not to have heard him speak that night.

How did we drift into that fatal conversation? I hardly remember. We talked first of the neighbourhood, then swayed away to books, then to people. Yes, that was how it came about. The Professor was speaking of a man whom we both knew in town, a curiously effeminate man, whose every thought and feeling seemed that of a woman. I said I disliked him, and condemned him for his woman's demeanour, his woman's mind; but the Professor thereupon joined issue with me.

"Pity the fellow, if you like," he uttered, in his rather strident voice; "but as to condemning him, I would as soon condemn a tadpole for not being a full-grown frog. His soul is beyond his power to manage, or even to coerce, you may depend upon it."

Having sipped his port, he drew a little nearer to me, and slightly dropped his voice.

"There would be less censure of individuals in this world," he said, "if people were only a little more thoughtful. These souls are like letters, and sometimes they are sealed up in the wrong envelope. For instance, a man's soul may be put into a woman's body, or *vice versâ*. It has been so in D——'s case. A mistake has been made."

"By Providence?" I interrupted, with, perhaps, just a *soupçon* of sarcasm in my voice.

The Professor smiled.

"Suppose we imitate Thomas Hardy, and say by the President of the Immortals, who makes sport with more humans than Tess," he answered. "Mistakes may be deliberate, just as their reverse may be accidental. Even a mighty power may condescend sometimes to a very practical joke. To a thinker the world is full of apple-pie beds, and cold wet sponges fall on us from at least half the doors we push open. The soul-juggleries of the before-mentioned President are very curious, but people will not realize that soul transference from body to body is as much a plain fact as the daily rising of the sun on one half of the world and its nightly setting on the other."

"Do you mean that souls pass on into the world again on the death of the particular body in which they have been for the moment confined?" I asked.

"Precisely: I have no doubt of it. Sometimes a woman's soul goes into a man's body; then the man acts woman, and people cry against him for effeminacy. The soul colours the body with actions, the body does not colour the soul, or not in the same degree."

"But we are not irresponsible. We can command ourselves."

The Professor smiled dryly.

"You think so?" he said. "I sometimes doubt it."

"And I doubt your theory of soul transference."

"That shows me—pardon the apparent impertinence—that you have never really examined the soul question with any close attention. Do you suppose that D—— really likes being so noticeably different from other men? Depend upon it, he has noticed in himself what we have noticed in him. Depend upon it, he has tried to be ordinary, and found it impossible. His soul manages him as a strong nature manages a weak one, and his soul is a female, not a male. For souls have sexes, otherwise what would be the sense of talking about wedded souls? I have no doubt whatever of the truth of reincarnation on earth. Souls go on and on following out their object of development."

"You believe that every soul is reincarnated?"

" A certain number of times."

" That even in the animal world the soul of one animal passes into the body of another ? "

" Wait a minute. Now we are coming to something that tends to prove my theory true. Animals have souls, as you imply. Who can know them intimately and doubt it for an instant ? Souls as immortal—or as mortal—as ours. And their souls, too, pass on."

" Into other animals ? "

" Possibly. And eventually, in the process of development, into human beings."

I laughed, perhaps a little rudely. " My dear Professor, I thought that old notion was quite exploded in these modern scientific days."

" I found my beliefs upon my own minute observations," he said rather frigidly. " I notice certain animals masquerading—to some extent—as human beings, and I draw my own conclusions. If they happen to fit in at all with the conclusions of Pythagoras— or anyone else, for that matter—well and good. If not, I am not much concerned. Surely you notice the animal—and not merely the animal, but definite animals— reproduced in man. There are men whose

whole demeanour suggests the monkey. I
have met women who in manner, appearance,
and even character, were intensely like cats."

I uttered a slight exclamation, which did
not interrupt him.

"Now, I have made a minute study of
cats. Of all animals they interest me the
most. They have less apparent intensity,
less uttered passion, than dogs, but in my
opinion more character. Their subtlety is
extraordinary, their sensitiveness wonderful.
Will you understand me when I say that all
dogs are men, all cats women? That remark
expresses the difference between them."

He paused a moment.

"Go on—go on," I said, leaning forward,
with my eyes fixed upon his keen, puckered
face.

He seemed pleased with my suddenly-
aroused interest.

"Cats are as subtle and as difficult to
understand as the most complex woman, and
almost as full of intuitions. If they have
been well treated, there is often a certain
gracious, condescending suavity in their demeanour at first, even towards a total stranger ; but if that stranger is ill disposed toward
them, they seem instinctively to read his soul,
and they are in arms directly. Yet they dis-

semble their fears in a cold indifference and
reserve. They do not take action : they
merely abstain from action. They withdraw
the soul that has peeped out, as they can
withdraw their claws into the pads upon their
feet. They do not show fight as a dog might,
they do not become aggressive, nor do they
whine and put their tails between their legs.
They are simply on guard, watchful, mistrust-
ful. Is not all this woman ? "

" Possibly," I answered, with a painful
effort to assume indifference.

" A woman intuitively knows who is her
friend and who is her enemy—so long, at
least, as her heart is not engaged; then she
runs wild, I allow. A woman—— But I need
not pursue the parallel. Besides, perhaps it
is scarcely to the point, for my object is not
to bolster up an absurd contention that all
women have the souls of cats. No ; but I
have met women so strangely like cats that
their souls have, as I said before souls do,
coloured their bodies in actions. They have
had the very look of cats in their faces.
They have moved like them. Their demeanour has been patently and strongly feline.
Now, I see nothing ridiculous in the assump-
tion that such women's bodies may contain
souls—in process of development, of course—

that formerly were merely cat souls, but that are now gaining humanity gradually, are working their way upwards in the scale. After all, we are not so much above the animals, and in our lapses we often become merely animals. The soul retrogrades for the moment."

He paused again and looked at me. I was biting my lips, and my glass of wine was untouched. He took my agitation as a compliment, I suppose, for he smiled and said:

"Are you in process of conversion?"

I half shook my head. Then I said, with an effort: "It is a curious and interesting idea, of course. But there is much to explain. Now, I should like to ask you this: Do you—do you believe that a soul, if it passes on as you think, carries its memory with it, its memory of former loves and—and hates? Say that a cat's soul goes to a woman's body, and that the cat has been—has been—well, tortured—possibly killed, by someone—say some man, long ago, would the woman, meeting that man, remember and shrink from him?"

"That is a very interesting and curious problem, and one which I do not pretend to have solved. I can, therefore, only suggest what might be, what seems to me reasonable.

I do not believe that the woman would remember positively, but I think she might have an intuition about the man. Our intuitions are, perhaps, sometimes only the fragmentary recollections of our souls, of what formerly happened to them when in other bodies. Why, otherwise, should we sometimes conceive an ardent dislike of some stranger—charming to all appearance—of whom we know no evil, whom we have never heard of nor met before ? Intuitions, so called, are often only tattered memories. And these intuitions might, I should fancy, be strengthened, given body, robustness, by associations —of place, for example. Cats become intensely attached to localities, to certain spots, a particular house or garden, a particular fireside, apart from the people who may be there. Possibly, if the man and the woman of whom you speak could be brought together in the very place where the torture and death occurred, the dislike of the woman might deepen into positive hatred. It would, however, be always unreasoning hatred, I think, and even quite unaccountable to herself. Still——"

But here Lord Melchester rose from the table. The conversations broke into fragments. I felt that I was pale to the lips.

We passed into the drawing-room. The ladies were grouped together at one end, near the piano. Margot was among them. She was, as usual, dressed in white, and round the bottom of her gown there was an edging of snow-white fur. As we came in, she moved away from the piano to a sofa at some distance, and sank down upon it. Professor Black, who had entered the room at my side, seized my arm gently.

"Now, that lady," he whispered in my ear—"I don't know who she may be, but she is intensely cat-like. I observed it before dinner. Did you notice the way she moved just then—the soft, yielding, easy manner in which she sat down, falling at once, quite naturally, into a charming pose? And her china-blue eyes are——"

"She is my wife, Professor," I interrupted harshly.

He looked decidedly taken aback.

"I beg your pardon; I had no idea. I did not enter the drawing-room to-night till after you arrived. I believed that lady was one of my fellow-guests in the house. Let me congratulate you. She is very beautiful."

And then he mingled rather hastily in the group near the piano.

The man is mad, I know—mad as a hatter

on one point, like so many clever men. He
sees the animal in every person he meets
just because his preposterous theory inclines
him to do so. Having given in his adherence to it, he sees facts not as they are, but
as he wishes them to be; but he shall not
carry me with him. The theory is his, not
mine. It does not hold water for a moment.
I can laugh at it now, but that night I confess it did seize me for the time being. I
could scarcely talk; I found myself watching Margot with a terrible intentness, and I
found myself agreeing with the Professor to
an extent that made me marvel at my own
previous blindness.

There was something strangely feline
about the girl I had married—the soft, white
girl who was becoming terrible to me, dear
though she still was and must always be.
Her movements had the subtle, instinctive
and certain grace of a cat's. Her cushioned
step, which had often struck me before, was
like the step of a cat. And those china-blue
eyes! A sudden cold seemed to pass over
me as I understood why I had recognised
them when I first met Margot. They were
the eyes of the animal I had tortured, the
animal I had killed. Yes, but that proved
nothing, absolutely nothing. Many people

had the eyes of animals—the soft eyes of
dogs, the furtive, cruel eyes of tigers. I had
known such people. I had even once had an
affair with a girl who was always called the
shot partridge, because her eyes were supposed to be like those of a dying bird. I
tried to laugh to myself as I remembered
this. But I felt cold, and my senses seemed
benumbed as by a great horror. I sat like a
stone, with my eyes fixed upon Margot, trying painfully to read into her all that the
words of Professor Black had suggested to
me—trying, but with the wish not to succeed.

I was roused by Lady Melchester, who
came toward me asking me to do something,
I forget now what. I forced myself to be
cheerful, to join in the conversation, to seem at
my ease; but I felt like one oppressed with
nightmare, and I could scarcely withdraw my
eyes from the sofa where my wife was sitting.
She was talking now to Professor Black, who
had just been introduced to her; and I felt a
sudden fury in my heart as I thought that he
was perhaps dryly, coldly, studying her, little
knowing what issues—far-reaching, it might
be, in their consequences—hung upon the
truth or falsehood of his strange theory.
They were talking earnestly, and presently it
occurred to me that he might be imbuing

Margot with his pernicious doctrines, that he might be giving her a knowledge of her own soul which now she lacked. The idea was insupportable. I broke off abruptly the conversation in which I was taking part, and hurried over to them with an impulse which must have astonished anyone who took note of me. I sat down on a chair, drew it forward almost violently, and thrust myself in between them.

"What are you two talking about?" I said, roughly, with a suspicious glance at Margot.

The Professor looked at me in surprise.

"I was instructing your wife in some of the mysteries of salmon-fishing," he said. "She tells me you have a salmon-river running through your grounds."

I laughed uneasily.

"So you are a fisherman as well as a romantic theorist!" I said, rather rudely. "How I wish I were as versatile! Come, Margot, we must be going now. The carriage ought to be here."

She rose quietly and bade the Professor good-night; but as she glanced up at me, in rising, I fancied I caught a new expression in her eyes. A ray of determination, of set purpose, mingled with the gloomy fire of their despair.

As soon as we were in the carriage I spoke, with a strained effort at ease and the haphazard tone which should mask furtive cross-examination.

"Professor Black is an interesting man," I said.

"Do you think so?" she answered from her dark corner.

"Surely. His intellect is really alive. Yet, with all his scientific knowledge and his power of eliciting facts and elucidating them, he is but a featherheaded man." I paused, but she made no answer. "Do you not think so?"

"How can I tell?" she replied. "We only talked about fishing. He managed to make that topic a pleasant one."

Her tone was frank. I felt relieved.

"He is exceedingly clever," I said, heartily, and we relapsed into silence.

When we reached home, and Margot had removed her cloak, she came up to me and laid her hand on my arm.

So unaccustomed was her touch now that I was startled. She was looking at me with a curious, steady smile—an unwavering smile that chilled instead of warming me.

"Ronald," she said, "there has been a breach between us. I have been the cause

9

of it. I should like to—to heal it. Do you still love me as you did?"

I did not answer immediately; I could not. Her voice, schooled as it was, seemed somehow at issue with the words she uttered. There was a desperate, hard note in it that accorded with that enigmatic smile of the mouth.

It roused a cold suspicion within me that I was close to a masked battery. I shrank physically from the touch of her hand.

She waited with her eyes upon me. Our faces were lit tremblingly by the flames of the two candles we held.

At last I found a voice.

"Can you doubt it?" I asked.

She drew a step nearer.

"Then let us resume our old relations," she said.

"Our old relations?"

"Yes."

I shuddered as if a phantom stole by me. I was seized with horror.

"To-night? It is not possible!"

"Why?" she said, still with that steady smile of the mouth.

"Because—because I don't know—I—— To-morrow it shall be as of old, Margot— to-morrow. I promise you."

"Very well. Kiss me, dear."

I forced myself to touch her lips with mine.

Which mouth was the colder?

Then, with that soft, stealthy step of hers, she vanished towards her room. I heard the door close gently.

I listened. The key was not turned in the lock.

This sudden abandonment by Margot of the fantastic precautions I had almost become accustomed to filled me with a nameless dread.

That night I fastened my door for the first time.

IV.

FRIDAY NIGHT, *November 6th.*

I FASTENED my door, and when I went to bed lay awake for hours listening. A horror was upon me then which has not left me since for a moment, which may never leave me. I shivered with cold that night, the cold born of sheer physical terror. I knew that I was shut up in the house with a soul bent on unreasoning vengeance, the soul of the animal which I had killed prisoned in the body of the woman I had married. I was sick with fear then. I am sick with fear now.

To-night I am so tired. My eyes are heavy and my head aches. No wonder. I have not slept for three nights. I have not dared to sleep.

This strange revolution in my wife's conduct, this passionless change—for I felt instinctively that warm humanity had nothing to do with the transformation—took place three nights ago. These three last days Margot has been playing a part. With what object ?

When I sat down to this gray record of two souls—at once dreary and fantastic as it would seem, perhaps, to many—I desired to reassure myself, to write myself into sweet reason, into peace.

I have tried to accomplish the impossible. I feel that the wildest theory may be the truest, after all—that on the borderland of what seems madness, actuality paces.

Every remembrance of my mind confirms the truth first suggested to me by Professor Black.

I know Margot's object now.

The soul of the creature that I tortured, that I killed, has passed into the body of the woman whom I love; and that soul, which once slept in its new cage, is awake now, watching, plotting perhaps. Unconsciously to itself, it recognises me.   It stares out upon me with eyes in which the dull terror deepens to hate; but it does not understand why it fears—why, in its fear, it hates.   Intuition has taken the place of memory.   The change of environment has killed recollection, and has left instinct in its place.

Why did I ever sit down to write?   The recalling of facts has set the seal upon my despair.

Instinct only woke in Margot when I brought her to the place the soul had known in the years when it looked out upon the world from the body of an animal.

That first day on the terrace instinct stirred in its sleep, opened its eyes, gazed forth upon me wonderingly, inquiringly.

Margot's faint remembrance of the terrace walk, of the flower-pots, of the grass borders where the cat had often stretched itself in the sun, her eagerness to see the chamber of death, her stealthy visits to that chamber, her growing uneasiness, deepening to acute apprehension, and finally to a deadly malignity —all lead me irresistibly to one conclusion.

The animal's soul within her no longer merely shrinks away in fear of me.   It has grown sinister.   It lies in ambush, full of a cold, a stealthy intention.

That curious, abrupt change in Margot's demeanour from avoidance to invitation marked the subtle, inward development of feeling, the silent passage from sensation only towards action.

Formerly she feared me.   Now I must fear her.

The soul, crouching in its cage, shows its teeth.   It is compassing my destruction.

The woman's body twitches with desire to avenge the death of the animal's.

I feel that it is only waiting the moment to spring ; and the inherent love of life breeds in me a physical fear of it as of a subtle enemy.   For even if the soul is brave, the body dreads to die, and seems at moments to possess a second soul, purely physical, that cries out childishly against pain, against death.

Then, too, there is a cowardice of the imagination that can shake the strongest heart, and this resurrection from the dead, from the murdered, appals my imagination.   That what I thought I had long since slain should have companioned me so closely when I knew it not !

I am sick with fear, physical and mental.

Two days ago, when I unlocked my bedroom door in the morning, and saw the autumn sunlight streaming in through the leaded panes of the hall windows, and heard the river dancing merrily down the gully among the trees that will soon be quite bare and naked, I said to myself: "You have been mad. Your mind has been filled with horrible dreams, that have transformed you into a coward and your wife into a demon. Put them away from you."

I looked across the gully. A clear, cold, thin light shone upon the distant mountains. The cloud stacks lay piled above the Scawfell range. The sky was a sheet of faded turquoise. I opened the window for a moment. The air was dry and keen. How sweet it was to feel it on my face!

I went down to the breakfast-room. Margot was moving about it softly, awaiting me. In her white hands were letters. They dropped upon the table as she stole up to greet me. Her lips were set tightly together, but she lifted them to kiss me.

How close I came to my enemy as our mouths touched! Her lips were colder than the wind.

Now that I was with her, my momentary sensation of acute relief deserted me. The horror that oppressed me returned.

I could not eat—I could only make a pretence of doing so; and my hand trembled so excessively that I could scarcely raise my cup from the table.

She noticed this, and gently asked me if I was ill.

I shook my head.

When breakfast was over, she said in a low, level voice :

" Ronald, have you thought over what I said last night ? "

" Last night ? " I answered, with an effort.

" Yes, about the coldness between us. I think I have been unwell, unhappy, out of sorts. You know that—that women are more subject to moods than men, moods they cannot always account for even to themselves. I have hurt you lately, I know. I am sorry. I want you to forgive me, to—to "—she paused a moment, and I heard her draw in her breath sharply—" to take me back into your heart again."

Every word, as she said it, sounded to me like a sinister threat, and the last sentence made my blood literally go cold in my veins.

I met her eyes. She did not withdraw hers ; they looked into mine. They were the blue eyes of the cat which I had held upon my knees years ago. I had gazed into them as a boy, and watched the horror and the fear dawn in them with a malignant triumph.

"I have nothing to forgive," I said in a broken, husky voice.

"You have much," she answered firmly. "But do not—pray do not bear malice."

"There is no malice in my heart—now," I said; and the words seemed like a cowardly plea for mercy to the victim of the past.

She lifted one of her soft white hands to my breast.

"Then it shall all be as it was before? And to-night you will come back to me?"

I hesitated, looking down. But how could I refuse? What excuse could I make for denying the request? Then I repeated mechanically:

"To-night I will come back to you."

A terrible, slight smile travelled over her face. She turned and left me.

I sat down immediately. I felt too unnerved to remain standing. I was giving way utterly to an imaginative horror that seemed to threaten my reason. In vain I tried to pull myself together. My body was in a cold sweat. All mastery of my nerves seemed gone.

I do not know how long I remained there, but I was aroused by the entrance of the butler. He glanced towards me in some obvious surprise, and this astonishment of a servant

acted upon me almost like a scourge. I
sprang up hastily.

"Tell the groom to saddle the mare," I
said. "I am going for a ride immediately."

Air, action, were what I needed to drive
this stupor away. I must get away from this
house of tears. I must be alone. I must
wrestle with myself, regain my courage, kill
the coward in me.

I threw myself upon the mare, and rode
out at a gallop towards the moors of Eskdale
along the lonely country roads.

All day I rode, and all day I thought of
that dark house, of that white creature awaiting my return, peering from the windows,
perhaps, listening for my horse's hoofs on
the gravel, keeping still the long vigil of vengeance.

My imagination sickened, fainted, as my
wearied horse stumbled along the shadowy
roads. My terror was too great now to be
physical. It was a terror purely of the spirit,
and indescribable.

To sleep with that white thing that waited
me! To lie in the dark by it! To know that
it was there, close to me!

If it killed me, what matter? It was to
live and to be near it, with it, that appalled
me.

The lights of the house gleamed out through the trees. I heard the sound of the river.

I got off my horse and walked furtively into the hall, looking round me.

Margot glided up to me immediately, and took my whip and hat from me with her soft, velvety white hands. I shivered at her touch.

At dinner her blue eyes watched me.

I could not eat, but I drank more wine than usual.

When I turned to go down to the smoking-room, she said: "Don't be very long, Ronald."

I muttered I scarcely know what words in reply. It was close on midnight before I went to bed. When I entered her room, shielding the light of the candle with my hand, she was still awake.

Nestling against the pillows, she stretched herself curiously and smiled up at me.

"I thought you were never coming, dear," she said.

I knew that I was very pale, but she did not remark it. I got into bed, but left the candle still burning.

Presently she said:

"Why don't you put the candle out?"

I looked at her furtively. Her face

seemed to me carved in stone, it was so rigid, so expressionless. She lay away from me at the extreme edge of the bed, sideways, with her hands toward me.

"Why don't you?" she repeated, with her blue eyes on me.

"I don't feel sleepy," I answered slowly.

"You never will while there is a light in the room," she said.

"You wish me to put it out?"

"Yes. How odd you are to-night, Ronald! Is anything the matter?"

"No," I answered; and I blew the light out.

How ghastly the darkness was!

I believed she meant to smother me in my sleep. I knew it. I determined to keep awake.

It was horrible to think that, as we lay there, she could see me all the time as if it were daylight.

The night wore on. She was quite silent and motionless. I lay listening.

It must have been towards morning when I closed my eyes, not because I was sleepy, but because I was so tired of gazing at blackness.

Soon after I had done this there was a stealthy movement in the bed.

"Margot, are you awake?" I instantly cried out sharply.

The movement immediately ceased. There was no reply.

When the light of dawn stole in at the window she seemed to be sleeping.

.   .   .   .   .   .

Last night I did not close my eyes once. She did not move.

She means to tire me out, and she has the strength to do it. To-night I feel so intensely heavy. Soon I must sleep, and then——

Shall I seek any longer to defend myself? Everything seems so inevitable, so beyond my power, like the working of an inexorable justice bent on visiting the sin of the father upon the child. For was not the cruel boy the father of the man?

And yet, is this tragedy inevitable? It cannot be. I will be a man. I will rise up and combat it. I will take Margot away from this house that her soul remembers, in which its body so long ago was tortured and slain, and she will—she must forget.

Instinct will sleep once more. It shall be so. I will have it so. I will strew poppies over her soul. I will take her far away from here, far away, to places where she will be once more as she has been.

To-morrow we will go. To-morrow——

.   .   .   .   .   .

Ah, that cry! Was it my own? I am suffocating! What was that? The horror of it! The pen has fallen from my hand. I must have slept; and I have dreamed. In my dream she stole upon me, that white thing! Her velvety hands were on my throat. The soul stared out from her eyes, the soul of the cat! Even her body, her woman's body, seemed to change at the moment of vengeance. She slowly strangled me, and as the breath died from me, and my failing eyes gazed at her, she was no longer woman at all, but something lithe and white and soft. Fur enveloped my throat. Those hands were claws. That breath on my face was the breath of an animal. The body had come back to companion the soul in its vengeance, the body of——

Ah, it was too horrible!

Can vengeance for the dead bring with it resurrection of the dead?

.   .   .   .   .   .

Hark! There is a voice calling to me from upstairs.

"Ronald, are you never coming? I am tired of waiting for you. Ronald!"

"Yes."

"Come to me!"

"And I must go."

.   .   .   .   .   .

Just at the glimmer of dawn the first pale shaft of the sun struck across a bed upon which lay the huddled and distorted corpse of a man. His head was sunk down in the pillows. His eyes, that could not see, stared towards the rising light. And from the open window of the chamber of death a woman in a white wrapper leaned out, watching eagerly with wide blue eyes the birds as they darted to and fro, rested on the climbing creepers, or circled above the gorge through which the river ran. Her set lips smiled. She looked like one calm, easy, and at peace. Presently an unwary sparrow perched on the trellis beneath the window just within her reach. Her white hand darted down softly, closed on the bird. She vanished from the window.

.   .   .   .   .   .

Can the dead hear? Did he catch the sound of her faint, continuous purring as she crouched with her prey upon the floor?

THE COLLABORATORS.

"WHY shouldn't we collaborate?" said Henley in his most matter-of-fact way, as Big.Ben gave voice to the midnight hour. "Everybody does it nowadays. Two heads may be really better than one, although I seldom believe in the truth of accepted sayings. Your head is a deuced good one, Andrew; but—now don't get angry—you are too excitable and too intense to be left quite to yourself, even in book-writing, much less in the ordinary affairs of life. I think you were born to collaborate, and to collaborate with me. You can give me everything I lack, and I can give you a little of the sense of humour, and act as a drag upon the wheel."

"None of the new humour, Jack; that shall never appear in a book with my name attached to it. Dickens I can tolerate. He is occasionally felicitous. The story of 'The Dying Clown,' for instance, crude as it is has a certain grim tragedy about it. But the new humour came from the pit, and should go—to the *Sporting Times.*"

"Now, don't get excited. The book is not in proof yet—perhaps never will be. You need not be afraid. My humour will probably be old enough. But what do you say to the idea?"

Andrew Trenchard sat for awhile in silent consideration. His legs were stretched out, and his slippered feet rested on the edge of the brass fender. A nimbus of smoke surrounded his swarthy features, his shock of black hair, his large, rather morose, dark eyes. He was a man of about twenty-five, with an almost horribly intelligent face, so observant that he tried people, so acute that he frightened them. His intellect was never for a moment at rest, unless in sleep. He devoured himself with his own emotions, and others with his analysis of theirs. His mind was always crouching to spring, except when it was springing. He lived an irregular life, and all horrors had a subtle fascination for him. As Henley had remarked, he possessed little sense of humour, but immense sense of evil and tragedy and sorrow. He seldom found time to calmly regard the drama of life from the front. He was always at the

stage-door, sending in his card, and request-
ing admittance behind the scenes. What was
on the surface only interested him in so far
as it indicated what was beneath, and in all
mental matters his normal procedure was
that of the disguised detective. Stupid
people disliked him. Clever people dis-
trusted him while they admired him. The
mediocre suggested that he was liable to go
off his head, and the profound predicted for
him fame, tempered by suicide.

Most people considered him interesting,
and a few were sincerely attached to him.
Among these last was Henley, who had been
his friend at Oxford, and had taken rooms
in the same house with him in Smith's Square,
Westminster. Both the young men were
journalists. Henley, who, as he had acknowledged, possessed a keen sense of humour, and was not so much ashamed of it as
he ought to have been, wrote—very occasionally—for *Punch*, and more often for *Fun*,
was dramatic critic of a lively society paper,
and "did" the books—in a sarcastic vein—
for a very unmuzzled "weekly," that was
libellous by profession and truthful by over-
sight. Trenchard, on the other hand, wrote
a good deal of very condensed fiction, and
generally placed it; contributed brilliant

fugitive articles to various papers and magazines, and was generally spoken of by the inner circle of the craft as "a rising man," and a man to be afraid of. Henley was full of common-sense, only moderately introspective, facile, and vivacious. He might be trusted to tincture a book with the popular element, and yet not to spoil it; for his literary sense was keen, despite his jocular leaning toward the new humour. He lacked imagination; but his descriptive powers were racy, and he knew instinctively what was likely to take, and what would be caviare to the general.

Trenchard, as he considered the proposition now made to him, realized that Henley might supply much that he lacked in any book that was written with a view to popular success. There could be no doubt of it.

"But we should quarrel inevitably and doggedly," he said at last. "If I can not hold myself in, still less can I be held in. We should tear one another in pieces. When I write, I feel that what I write must be, however crude, however improper or horrible it may seem. You would want to hold me back."

"My dear boy, I should more than want to—I should do it. In collaboration, no man

can be a law unto himself. That must be
distinctly understood before we begin. I
don't wish to force the proposition on you.
Only we are both ambitious devils. We are
both poor. We are both determined to try a
book. Have we more chance of succeeding
if we try one together? I believe so. You
have the imagination, the grip, the stern
power to evolve the story, to make it seem inevitable, to force it step by step on its way.
I can lighten that way. I can plant a few
flowers—they shall not be peonies, I promise
you—on the roadside. And I can, and, what
is more, will, check you when you wish to
make the story impossibly horrible or fantastic to the verge of the insane. Now, you
needn't be angry. This book, if we write it,
has got to be a good book, and yet a book
that will bring grist to the mill. That is understood."

Andrew's great eyes flashed in the lamp-
light.

"The mill," he said. "Sometimes I feel
inclined to let it stop working. Who would
care if one wheel ceased to turn? There are
so many others."

"Ah, that's the sort of thing I shall cut out
of the book!" cried Henley, turning the soda-
water into his whisky with a cheerful swish.

"We will be powerful, but never morbid; tragic, if you like, but not without hope. We need not aspire too much; but we will not look at the stones in the road all the time. And the dunghills, in which those weird fowl, the pessimistic realists, love to rake, we will sedulously avoid. Cheer up, old fellow, and be thankful that you possess a corrective in me."

Trenchard's face lightened in a rare smile as, with a half-sigh, he said :

" I believe you are right, and that I need a collaborator, an opposite, who is yet in sympathy with me. Yes ; either of us might fail alone ; together we should succeed."

" *Will* succeed, my boy ! "

" But not by pandering to the popular taste," added Andrew in his most sombre tones, and with a curl of his thin, delicately-moulded lips. " I shall never consent to that."

" We will not call it pandering. But we must hit the taste of the day, or we shall look a couple of fools."

" People are always supposed to look fools when, for once, they are not fools," said Andrew.

" Possibly. But now our bargain is made. Strike hands upon it. Henceforth we are collaborators as well as friends."

Andrew extended his long, thin, feverish hand, and, as Henley held it for a moment, he started at the intense, vivid, abnormal personality its grasp seemed to reveal. To collaborate with Trenchard was to collaborate with a human volcano.

"And now for the germ of our book," he said, as the clock struck one. "Where shall we find it?"

Trenchard leaned forward in his chair, with his hands pressed upon the arms.

"Listen, and I will give it you," he said.

And, almost until the dawn and the wakening of the slumbering city, Henley sat and listened, and forgot that his pipe was smoked out, and that his feet were cold. Trenchard had strange powers, and could enthral as he could also repel.

.   .   .   .   .   .

"It is a weird idea, and it is very powerful," Henley said at last. "But you stop short at the critical moment. Have you not devised a *dénouement?*"

"Not yet. That is where the collaboration will come in. You must help me. We must talk it over. I am in doubt."

He got up and passed his hands nervously through his thick hair.

"My doubt has kept me awake so many

nights!" he said, and his voice was rather husky and worn.

Henley looked at him almost compassionately.

"How intensely you live in your fancies!"

"My fancies?" said Andrew, with a sudden harsh accent, and darting a glance of curious watchfulness upon his friend. "My —— Yes, yes. Perhaps I do. Perhaps I try to. Some people have souls that must escape from their environment, their miserable life-envelope, or faint. Many of us labour and produce merely to create an atmosphere in which we ourselves may breathe for awhile and be happy. Damn this London, and this lodging, and this buying bread with words! I must create for myself an atmosphere. I must be always getting away from what is, even if I go lower, lower. Ah! Well —but the *dénouement*. Give me your impressions."

Henley meditated for awhile. Then he said: "Let us leave it. Let us get to work; and in time, as the story progresses, it will seem inevitable. We shall see it in front of us, and we shall not be able to avoid it. Let us get to work"—he glanced at his watch and laughed—" or, rather, let us get to bed. It is past four. This way madness lies.

When we collaborate, we will write in the morning. Our book shall be a book of the dawn, and not of the darkness, despite its sombre theme."

" No, no ; it must be a book of the darkness."

" Of the darkness, then, but written in the dawn. Your tragedy tempered by my trust in human nature, and the power that causes things to right themselves. Good-night, old boy."

" Good-night."

When Henley had left the room, Trenchard sat for a moment with his head sunk low on his breast and his eyes half closed. Then, with a jerk, he gained his feet, went to the door, opened it, and looked forth on the deserted landing. He listened, and heard Henley moving to and fro in his bedroom. Then he shut the door, took off his smoking-coat, and bared his left arm. There was a tiny blue mark on it.

" What will the *dénouement* be ? " he whispered to himself, as he felt in his waistcoat pocket with a trembling hand.

II.

THE book was moving onward by slow degrees and with a great deal of discussion.

In those days Henley and Trenchard lived much with sported oaks. They were battling for fame. They were doing all they knew. Literary gatherings missed them. First nights knew them no more. The grim intensity that was always characteristic of Trenchard seemed in some degree communicated to Henley. He began to more fully understand what the creating for one's self of an atmosphere meant. The story he and his friend were fashioning fastened upon him like some strange, determined shadow from the realms of real life, gripped him more and more closely, held him for long spells of time in a new and desolate world. For the book so far was a deepening tragedy, and although, at times, Henley strove to resist the paramount influence which the genius of Trenchard began to exercise over him, he found himself comparatively impotent, unable to shed gleams of popular light upon the darkness of the pages. The power of the tale was undoubted. Henley felt that it was a big thing that they two were doing; but would it be a popular thing—a money-making thing? That was the question. He sometimes wished with all his heart they had chosen a different subject to work their combined talent upon.

The germ of the work seemed only capable of tragic treatment, if the book were to be artistic. Their hero was a man of strong intellect, of physical beauty, full at first of the joy of life, chivalrous, a believer in the innate goodness of human nature. Believing in goodness, he believed also ardently in influence. In fact, he was a worshipper of influence, and his main passion was to seize upon the personalities of others, and impose his own personality upon them. He loved to make men and women see with his eyes and hear with his ears, adopt his theories as truth, take his judgment for their own. All that he thought *was*—to him. He never doubted himself, therefore he could not bear that those around him should not think with him, act towards men and women as he acted, face life as he faced it. Yet he was too subtle ever to be dogmatic. He never shouted in the market-place. He led those with whom he came in contact as adroitly as if he had been evil, and to the influence of others he was as adamant.

Events brought into his life a woman, complex, subtle too, with a naturally noble character and fine understanding, a woman who, like so many women, might have been anything, and was far worse than nothing—a hopeless, helpless slave, the victim of the morphia habit, which had gradually degraded her, driven her through sloughs of immorality, wrecked a professional career which at one time had been almost great, shattered her constitution, though not all her still curious beauty, and ruined her, to all intents and purposes, body and soul. The man and the woman met, and in a flash the man saw what she had been, what she might have been, what, perhaps, in spite of all, she still was, somewhere, somehow. In her horrible degradation, in her dense despair, she fascinated him. He could only see the fire bursting out of the swamp. He could only feel on his cheek the breath of the spring in the darkness of the charnel-house. He knew that she gave to him his great lifework. Her monstrous habit he simply could not comprehend. It was altogether as fantastic to him as absolute virtue sometimes seems to absolute vice. He looked upon it, and felt as little kinship with it as a saint might feel with a vampire. To him it was merely a hideous and extraordinary growth, which had fastened like a cancer upon a beautiful and wonderful body, and which must be cut out. He was profoundly interested.

He loved the woman. Seeing her governed entirely by a vice, he made the very common mistake of believing her to have a weak personality, easily falling, perhaps for that very reason as easily lifted to her feet. He resolved to save her, to devote all his powers, all his subtlety, all his intellect, all his strong force of will, to weaning this woman from her fatal habit. She was a married woman, long ago left, to kill herself if she would, by the husband whose happiness she had wrecked. He took her to live with him. For her sake he defied the world, and set himself to do angel's work when people believed him at the devil's. He resolved to wrap her, to envelop her in his influence, to enclose her in his strong personality. Here, at last, was a grand, a noble opportunity for the legitimate exercise of his master passion. He was confident of victory.

But his faith in himself was misplaced. This woman, whom he thought so weak, was yet stronger than he. Although he could not influence her, he began to find that she could influence him. At first he struggled with her vice, which he could not understand. He thought himself merely horrified at it; then he began to lose the horror in wonder at its power. Its virility, as it were, fascinated him just a little. A vice so overwhelmingly strong seemed to him at length almost glorious, almost God-like. There was a sort of humanity about it. Yes, it was like a being who lived and who conquered.

The woman loved him, and he tried to win her from it; but her passion for it was greater than her passion for him, greater than had been her original passion for purity, for health, for success, for homage, for all lovely and happiness-making things. Her passion for it was so great that it roused the man's curiosity at last; it made him hold his breath, and stand in awe, and desire furtively to try just once for himself what its dominion was like, to test its power as one may test the power of an electric battery. He dared not do this openly, for fear the fact of his doing so might drive the woman still farther on the downward path. So in secret he tasted the fascinations of her vice, once—and again —and yet again. But still he struggled for her while he was ceasing to struggle for himself. Still he combated for her the foe who was conquering him. Very strange, very terrible was his position in that London house with her, isolated from the world. For his friends had dropped him. Even those who were not scandalized at his relations with this woman had ceased to come near him. They found him blind and deaf to the ordinary interests of life. He never went out anywhere, unless occasionally with her to some theatre. He never invited anyone to come and see him. At first the woman absorbed all his interest, all his powers of love—and then at last the woman and her vice, which was becoming his too. By degrees he sank lower and lower, but he never told the woman the truth, and he still urged her to give up her horrible habit, which now he loved. And she laughed in his face, and asked him if a human creature who had discovered a new life would be likely to give it up. "A new death," he murmured, and then, looking in a mirror near to him, saw his lips curved in the thin, pale smile of the hypocrite.

.   .   .   .   .   .

So far the two young men had written. They worked hard, but their industry was occasionally interrupted by the unaccountable laziness of Andrew, who, after toiling with unremitting fury for some days, and scarcely getting up from his desk, would disappear, and perhaps not return for several nights. Henley remonstrated with him, but in vain.

"But what do you do, my dear fellow?" he asked. "What becomes of you?"

"I go away to think out what is coming. The environment I seek helps me," answered Andrew, with a curious, gleaming smile. "I return full of fresh copy."

This was true enough. He generally mysteriously departed when the book was beginning to flag, and on his reappearance he always set to work with new vigour and confidence.

"It seems to me," Henley said, "that it will be your book after all, not mine. It is your plot, and when I think things over I find that every detail is yours. You insisted on the house where the man and the woman hid themselves being on the Chelsea Embankment. You invented the woman, her character, her appearance. You named her Olive Beauchamp."

"Olive Beauchamp," Andrew repeated, with a strange lingering over the two words, which he pronounced in a very curious voice that trembled, as if with some keen emotion, love or hate. "Yes; I named her as you say."

"Then, as the man in the play remarks, 'Where do I come in?'" Henley asked, half laughing, half vexed. "Upon my word, I shall have some compunction in putting my name below yours on the title-page when the book is published, if it ever is."

Andrew's lips twitched once or twice uneasily. Then he said, "You need not have any such compunction. The greatest chapter will probably be written by you."

· "Which chapter do you mean?"

"That which winds the story up—that which brings the whole thing to its legitimate conclusion. You must write the *dénouement*."

"I doubt if I could. And then we have not even now decided what it is to be."

"We need not bother about that yet. It will come. Fate will decide it for us."

"What do you mean, Andrew? How curiously you talk about the book sometimes —so precisely as if it were true!"

Trenchard smiled again, struck a match, and lit his pipe.

"It seems true to me—when I am writing it," he answered. "I have been writing it these last two days and nights when I have been away, and now I can go forward, if you agree to the new development which I suggest."

It was night. He had been absent for some days, and had just returned. Henley, meanwhile, had been raging because the book had come to a complete standstill. He himself could do nothing at it, since they had reached a dead-lock, and had not talked over any new scenes, or mutually decided upon the turn events were now to take. He felt rather cross and sore.

"*You* can go forward," he said: "yes, after your holiday. You might at least tell me when you are going."

"I never know myself," Andrew said rather sadly.

He was looking very white and worn, and his eyes were heavy.

"But I have thought some fresh material out. My idea is this: The man now becomes such a complete slave to the morphia habit that concealment of the fact is scarcely possible. And, indeed, he ceases to desire to conceal it from the woman. The next scene will be an immensely powerful one—that in which he tells her the truth."

"You do not think it would be more natural if she found it out against his will? It seems to me that what he had concealed so long he would try to hide for ever."

"No," Andrew said emphatically; "that would not be so."

"But——"

"Look here," the other interrupted, with some obvious irritability; "let me tell you what I have conceived, and raise any objec-

11

tions afterwards if you wish to raise them. He would tell her the truth himself. He would almost glory in doing so. That is the nature of the man. We have depicted his pride in his own powers, his temptation, his struggle—his fall, as it would be called——"

"As it would be called."

"Well, well!—his fall, then. And now comes the moment when his fall is complete. He bends the neck finally beneath his tyrant, and then he goes to the woman and he tells her the truth."

"But explain matters a little more. Do you mean that he is glad, and tells almost with triumph; or that he is appalled, and tells her with horror?"

"Ah! That is where the power of the scene lies. He is appalled. He is like a man plunged at last into hell without hope of future redemption. He tells her the truth with horror."

"And she?"

"It is she who triumphs. Look here: it will be like this."

Andrew leaned forward across the table that stood between their two worn armchairs. His thin, feverish-looking hands, with the fingers strongly twisted together, rested upon it. His dark eyes glittered with excitement.

"It will be like this. It is evening—a dark, dull evening, like the day before yesterday, closing in early, throttling the afternoon prematurely, as it were. A drizzling rain falls softly, drenching everything—the sodden leaves of the trees on the Embankment, the road, which is heavy with clinging yellow mud, the stone coping of the wall that skirts the river.

"And the river heaves along. Its gray, dirty waves are beaten up by a light, chilly wind, and chase the black barges with a puny, fretful, sinister fury, falling back from their dark, wet sides with a hiss of baffled hatred. Yes, it is dreary weather.

"Do you know, Henley, as I know, the strange, subtle influence of certain kinds of weather? There are days on which I could do great deeds merely because of the way the sun is shining. There are days, there are evenings, when I could commit crimes merely because of the way the wind is whispering, the river is sighing, the dingy night is clustering around me. There can be an angel in the weather, or there can be a devil. On this evening I am describing there is a devil in the night!

"The lights twinkle through the drizzling rain, and they are blurred, as bright eyes are blurred, and made dull and ugly, by tears. Two or three cabs roll slowly by the houses on the Embankment. A few people hurry past along the slippery, shining pavement. But as the night closes in there is little life outside those tall, gaunt houses that are so near the river! And in one of those houses the man comes down to the woman to tell her the truth.

"There is a devil in the weather that night, as I said, and that devil whispers to the man, and tells him that it is now his struggle must end finally, and the new era of unresisted yielding to the vice begin. In the sinister darkness, in the diminutive, drenching mist of rain, he speaks, and the man listens, and bows his head and answers 'yes!' It is over. He has fallen finally. He is resolved, with a strange, dull obstinacy that gives him a strange, dull pleasure—do you see?—to go down to the room below, and tell the woman that she has conquered him—that his power of will is a reed which can be crushed—that henceforth there shall be two victims instead of one. He goes down."

Andrew paused a moment. His lips were twitching again. He looked terribly excited. Henley listened in silence. He had lost all wish to interrupt.

"He goes down into the room below where the woman is, with her dark hair, and her dead-white face, and her extraordinary eyes—large, luminous, sometimes dull and without expression, sometimes dilated, and with an unnatural life staring out of them. She is on the sofa near the fire. He sits down beside her. His head falls into his hands, and at first he is silent. He is thinking how he will tell her. She puts her soft, dry hand on his, and she says: 'I am very tired to-night. Do not begin your evening sermon. Let me have it to-morrow. How you must love me to be so persistent! and how you must love me to be so stupid as to think that your power of will can break the power of such a habit as mine!'

"Then he draws his hand away from hers, and he lifts his head from his hands, and he tells her the truth. She leans back against a cushion staring at him in silence, devouring him with her eyes, which have become very bright and eager and searching. Presently he stops.

"'Go on,' she says, 'go on. Tell me more. Tell me all you feel. Tell me how the habit stole upon you, and came to you again and again, and stayed with you. Tell me how you first liked it, and then loved it, and how it was something to you, and then much, and then everything. Go on! go on!'

"And he catches her excitement. He conceals nothing from her. All the hideous, terrible, mental processes he has been through, he details to her, at first almost' gloating over his own degradation. He even exaggerates, as a man exaggerates in telling a story to an eager auditor. He is carried away by her strange fury of listening. He lays bare his soul; he exposes its wounds; he sears them with red-hot irons for her to see. And then at last all is told. He can think of no more details. He has even embellished the abominable truth. So he is silent, and he looks at her."

"And what does she do?" asked Henley, with a catch in his voice as he spoke. Undoubtedly in relating a fictitious narrative Andrew had a quite abnormal power of making it appear true and real.

"She looks at him, and then she bursts out laughing. Her eyes shine with triumph. She is glad; she is joyous with the joy of a lost soul when it sees that other souls are irrevocably lost too; she laughs, and she says nothing."

"And the man?"

Andrew's eyes suddenly dilated. He

leaned forward and laid his hand on Henley's arm.

"Ah, the man! that is my great idea. As she laughs his heart is changed. His love for her suddenly dies. Its place is taken by hatred. He realizes then, for the first time, while he hears her laugh, what she has done to him. He knows that she has ruined him, and that she is proud of it—that she is rejoicing in having won him to destruction. He sees that his perdition is merely a feather in her cap. He hates her. Oh, how he hates her!—hates her!"

The expression on Andrew's face became terrible as he spoke—cruel, malignant, almost fiendish. Henley turned cold, and shook off his hand abruptly.

"That is horrible!" he said. "I object to that. The book will be one of unrelieved gloom."

"The book!" said Andrew.

"Yes. You behave really as if the story were true, as if everything in it were ordained —inevitable."

"It seems so to me; it is so. What must be, must be. If you are afraid of tragedy, you ought never to have joined me in starting upon such a story. Even what has never happened must be made to seem actual to be

successful. The art of fiction is to imitate
truth with absolute fidelity, not to travesty it.
In such circumstances the man's love would·
be changed to hatred."

"Yes, if the woman's demeanour were
such as you have described. But why should
she be so callous? 'I do not think that is
natural."

"You do not know the woman," began
Andrew harshly. Then he stopped speaking
abruptly, and a violent flush swept over his
face.

"I know her as well as you do, my dear
fellow," rejoined Henley, laughing. "How
you manage to live in your dreams! You
certainly do create an atmosphere for yourself with a vengeance, and for me too. I believe you have an abnormal quantity of elec-
tricity concealed about you somewhere, and
sometimes you give me a shock and carry me
out of myself. If this is collaboration, it is
really a farce. From the very first you have
had things all your own way. You have
talked me over to your view upon every sin-
gle occasion; but now I am going to strike.
I object to the conduct you have devised for
Olive. It will alienate all sympathy from
her; it is the behaviour of a devil."

"It is the behaviour of a woman," said

Andrew, with a cold cynicism that seemed to cut like a knife.

" How can you tell? How can you judge of women so surely ? "

" I study all strange phenomena, women among the rest."

" Have you ever met an Olive Beauchamp, then, in real life ? " said Henley.

The question was put more than half in jest; but Trenchard received it with a heavy frown.

" Don't let us quarrel about the matter," he said. " I can only tell you this ; and mind, Jack, I mean it. It is my unalterable resolve. Either the story must proceed upon the lines that I have indicated, or I cannot go on with it at all. It would be impossible for me to write it differently."

"And this is collaboration, is it ? " exclaimed the other, trying to force a laugh, though even his good-nature could scarcely stand Trenchard's trampling demeanour.

" I can't help it. I cannot be inartistic and untrue to Nature even for the sake of a friend."

" Thank you. Well, I have no desire to ruin your work, Andrew; but it is really useless for this farce to continue. Do what you like, and let us make no further pretence of collaborating. I cannot act as a drag upon such a wheel as yours. I will not any longer be a dead-weight upon you. Our temperaments evidently unfit us to be fellow-workers; and I feel that your strength and power are so undeniable that you may, perhaps, be able to carry this weary tragedy through, and by sheer force make it palatable to the public. I will protest no more; I will only cease any longer to pretend to have a finger in this literary pie."

Andrew's morose expression passed away like a cloud. He got up and laid his hand upon Henley's shoulder.

"You make me feel what a beast I am," he said. "But I can't help it. I was made so. Do forgive me, Jack. I have taken the bit between my teeth, I know. But—this story seems to me no fiction; it is a piece of life, as real to me as those stars I see through the window-pane are real to me—as my own emotions are real to me. Jack, this book has seized me. Believe me, if it is written as I wish, it will make an impression upon the world that will be great. The mind of the world is given to me like a sheet of blank paper. I will write upon it with my heart's blood. But "—and here his manner became strangely impressive, and his sombre, heavy

eyes gazed deeply into the eyes of his friend
—"remember this! You will finish this book.
I feel that; I know it. I cannot tell you
why. But so it is ordained. Let me write as
far as I can, Jack, and let me write as I will.
But do not let us quarrel. The book is ours,
not mine. And—don't—don't take away
your friendship from me."

The last words were said with an outburst
of emotion that was almost feminine in intensity. Henley felt deeply moved, for, as a
rule, Andrew's manner was not specially af-
fectionate, or even agreeable.

"It is all right, old fellow," he said, in
the embarrassed English manner which often
covers so much that might with advantage
be occasionally revealed. "Go on in your
own way. I believe you are a genius, and I
am only trying to clip the wings that may
carry you through the skies. Go on in your
own way, and consult me only when you feel
inclined."

Andrew took his hand and pressed it in
silence.

III.

It was some three weeks after this that
one afternoon Trenchard laid down his pen
at the conclusion of a chapter, and, getting

up, thrust his hands into his pockets and walked to the window.

The look-out was rather dreary. A gray sky leaned over the great, barrack-like church that gives an ecclesiastical flavour to Smith's Square. A few dirty sparrows fluttered above the gray pavement—feverish, unresting birds, Trenchard named them silently, as he watched their meaningless activity, their jerky, ostentatious deportment, with lack-lustre, yet excited, eyes. How gray everything looked, tame, colourless, indifferent! The light was beginning to fade stealthily out of things. The gray church was gradually becoming shadowy. The flying forms of the hurrying sparrows disappeared in the weary abysses of the air and sky. The sitting-room in Smith's Square was nearly dark now. Henley had gone out to a *matinée* at one of the theatres, so Trenchard was alone. He struck a match presently, lit a candle, carried it over to his writing-table, and began to examine the littered sheets he had just been writing. The book was nearing its end. The tragedy was narrowing to a point. Trenchard read the last paragraph which he had written:

"He hardly knew that he lived, except during those many hours when, plunged in dreams, he allowed, nay, forced, life to leave him for awhile. He had sunk to depths below even those which Olive had reached. And the thought that she was ever so little above him haunted him like a spectre impelling him to some mysterious deed. When he was not dreaming, he was dwelling upon this idea which had taken his soul captive. It seemed to be shaping itself towards an act. Thought was the ante-room through which he passed to the hall where Fate was sitting, ready to give him audience. He traversed this ante-room, which seemed lined with fantastic and terrible pictures, at first with lagging footfalls. But at length he laid his hand upon the door that divided him from Fate."

. . . .

And when he had read the final words he gathered the loose sheets together with his long, thin fingers, and placed them one on the top of the other in a neat pile. He put them into a drawer which contained other unfinished manuscripts, shut the drawer, locked it, and carried the key to Henley's room. There he scribbled some words on a bit of notepaper, wrapped the key in it, and inclosed it in an envelope on which he wrote Henley's name. Then he put on his overcoat, descended the narrow stairs, and opened the front-door. The landlady heard him, and screamed from the basement to know if he would be in to dinner.

"I shall not be in at all to-night," he answered, in a hard, dry voice that travelled along the dingy passage with a penetrating distinctness. The landlady murmured to the slatternly maidservant an ejaculatory diatribe on the dissipatedness of young literary gentlemen as the door banged. Trenchard disappeared in the gathering darkness, and soon left Smith's Square behind him.

It chanced that day that, in the theatre, Henley encountered some ladies who carried him home to tea after the performance. They lived in Chelsea, and in returning to Smith's Square afterwards Henley took his way along the Chelsea Embankment. He always walked near to the dingy river when he could. The contrast of its life to the town's life through which it flowed had a perpetual fascination for him. In the early evening, too, the river presents many Doré effects. It is dim, mysterious, sometimes meretricious, with its streaks of light close to the dense shadows that lie under the bridges, its wailful, small waves licking the wharves, and bearing up the inky barges that look like the ferry-boat of the Styx. Henley loved to feel vivaciously despairing, and he hugged himself in the belief that the Thames at nightfall tinged his soul with a luxurious melancholy, the capacity for which was not far from rendering him a poet. So he took his way by the river. As he neared Cheyne Row, he saw in front of him the figure of a man leaning over the low stone wall, with his face buried in his hands. On hearing his approaching footsteps the man lifted himself up, turned round, and preceded him along the pavement with a sort of listless stride which seemed to Henley strangely familiar. He hastened his steps, and on coming closer recognised that the man was Trenchard; but, just as he was about to hail him, Trenchard crossed the road to one of the houses opposite, inserted a key in the door, and disappeared within, shutting the door behind him.

Henley paused a moment opposite to the house. It was of a dull red colour, and had a few creepers straggling helplessly about it, looking like a torn veil that can only partially conceal a dull, heavy face.

"Andrew seems at home here," he thought, gazing up at the blind, tall windows, which showed no ray of light. "I wonder——"

And then, still gazing at the windows, he

recalled the description of the house where Olive Beauchamp lived in their book.

"He took it from this," Henley said to himself. Yes, that was obvious. Trenchard had described the prison-house of despair, where the two victims of a strange, desolating habit shut themselves up to sink, with a curious minuteness. He had even devoted a paragraph to the tall iron gate, whose round handle he had written of as " bald, and exposed to the wind from the river, the paint having long since been worn off it." In the twilight Henley bent down and examined the handle of the gate. The paint seemed to have been scraped from it.

"How curiously real that book has become to me!" he muttered. "I could almost believe that if I knocked upon that door, and was let in, I should find Olive Beauchamp stretched on a couch in the room that lies beyond those gaunt, shuttered windows."

He gave a last glance at the house, and as he did so he fancied that he heard a slight cry come from it to him. He listened attentively and heard nothing more. Then he walked away toward home.

When he reached his room, he found upon his table the envelope which Trenchard had directed to him. He opened it, and unwrapped the key from the inclosed sheet of notepaper, on which were written these words:

"DEAR JACK,

"I am off again. And this time I can't say when I shall be back. In any case, I have completed my part of the book, and leave the finishing of it in your hands. This is the key of the drawer in which I have locked the manuscript. You have not seen most of the last volume. Read it, and judge for yourself whether the *dénouement* can be anything but utterly tragic. I will not outline to you what I have thought of for it. If you have any difficulty about the *finale*, I shall be able to help you with it even if you do not see me again for some time. By the way, what nonsense that saying is, 'Dead men tell no tales!' Half the best tales in the world are told, or at least completed, by dead men.

"Yours ever,

A. T."

Henley laid this note down and turned cold all over. It was the concluding sentence which had struck a chill through his heart. He took the key in his hand, went down to Trenchard's room, unlocked the drawer in his writing-table, and took out the manuscript. What did Andrew mean by that sinister sentence? A tale completed by a dead man! Henley sat down by the fire with the manuscript in his hands and began to read. He was called away to dinner; but immediately afterward he returned to his task, and till late into the night his glance travelled down the closely-written sheets one after the other, until the light from the candles grew blurred and indistinct, and his eyes ached. But still he read on. The power and gloom of Andrew's narrative held him in a vice, and then he was searching for a clue in the labyrinth of words. At last he came to the final paragraph, and then to the final sentence:

" But at length he laid his hand upon the door that divided him from Fate."

Henley put the sheet down carefully upon the table. It was three o'clock in the morning, and the room seemed full of a strange, breathless cold, the peculiar chilliness that precedes the dawn. The fire was burning brightly enough, yet the warmth it emitted scarcely seemed to combat the frosty air that penetrated from without, and Henley shivered as he rose from his seat. His brows were drawn together, and he was thinking deeply. A light seemed slowly struggling into his soul. That last sentence of Trenchard's connected itself with what he had seen in the afternoon on the Chelsea Embankment. " He laid his hand upon the door that divided him from Fate."

A strange idea dawned in Henley's mind, an idea which made many things clear to him. Yet he put it away, and sat down again to read the unfinished book once more. Andrew had carried on the story of the man's growing hatred of the woman whom he had tried to rescue, until it had developed into a deadly fury, threatening immediate action. Then he had left the *dénouement* in Henley's hands. He had left it ostensibly in Henley's hands, but the latter, reading the manuscript again with intense care, saw that matters had been so contrived that the knot of the novel could only be cut by murder. As it had been written, the man must inevitably murder the woman. And Andrew ? All through the night Henley thought of him as he had last seen him, opening the door of the red house with the tattered creepers climbing over it.

At last, when it was dawn, he went up to bed tired out, after leaving a written direction to the servant not to call him in the morning. When he awoke and looked at his watch it was past two o'clock in the afternoon. He sprang out of bed, dressed, and after a hasty meal, half breakfast, half lunch, set out towards Chelsea. The day was bright and cold. The sun shone on the river and sparkled on the windows of the houses on the Embankment. Many people were about, and they looked cheerful. The weight of depression that had settled upon Henley was lifted. He thought of the strange, yet illuminating, idea that had occurred to him in the night, and now, in broad daylight, it seemed clothed in absurdity. He laughed at it. Yet he quickened his steps toward the red house with the tarnished iron gate and the tattered creepers.

But long before he reached it he met a boy sauntering along the thoroughfare and shouting newspapers. He sang out unflinchingly in the gay sunshine, "Murder! Murder!" and between his shouts he whistled a music-hall song gaily in snatches. Henley stopped him and bought a paper. He opened the paper in the wind, which seemed striving to prevent him, and cast his eyes over the middle pages. Then suddenly he dropped it to the ground with a white face, and falteringly signed to a cabman. The *dénouement* was written. The previous night, in a house on the Chelsea Embankment, a woman had been done to death, and the murderer had crept out and thrown himself into the gray, hurrying river.

The woman's name was Olive Beauchamp.

THE END.

SLEEPING FIRES. By GEORGE GISSING, author of "In the Year of Jubilee," "Eve's Ransom," etc. 16mo. Cloth, 75 cents.

In this striking story the author has treated an original motive with rare self-command and skill. His book is most interesting as a story, and remarkable as a literary performance.

STONEPASTURES. By ELEANOR STUART. 16mo. Cloth, 75 cents.

"This is a strong bit of good literary workmanship. . . . The book has the value of being a real sketch of our own mining regions, and of showing how, even in the apparently dull round of work, there is still material for a good bit of literature."—*Philadelphia Ledger.*

COURTSHIP BY COMMAND. By M. M. BLAKE. 16mo. Cloth, 75 cents.

"A bright, moving study of an unusually interesting period in the life of Napoleon, . . . deliciously told; the characters are clearly, strongly, and very delicately modeled, and the touches of color most artistically done. 'Courtship by Command' is the most satisfactory Napoleon *bonne-bouche* we have had."—*New York Commercial Advertiser.*

THE WATTER'S MOU'. By BRAM STOKER. 16mo. Cloth, 75 cents.

"Here is a tale to stir the most sluggish nature. . . . It is like standing on the deck of a wave-tossed ship; you feel the soul of the storm go into your blood."—*New York Home Journal.*

MASTER AND MAN. By Count LEO TOLSTOY. With an Introduction by W. D. HOWELLS. 16mo. Cloth, 75 cents.

"Crowded with these characteristic touches which mark his literary work."—*Public Opinion.*

"Reveals a wonderful knowledge of the workings of the human mind, and it tells a tale that not only stirs the emotions, but gives us a better insight into our own hearts."—*San Francisco Argonaut.*

THE ZEIT-GEIST. By L. DOUGALL, author of "The Mermaid," "Beggars All," etc. 16mo. Cloth, 75 cents.

"One of the best of the short stories of the day."—*Boston Journal.*

"One of the most remarkable novels of the year."—*New York Commercial Advertiser.*

"Powerful in conception, treatment, and influence."—*Boston Globe.*

New York: D. APPLETON & CO., 72 Fifth Avenue.

BY S. R. CROCKETT.

*C*LEG KELLY, ARAB OF THE CITY. His Progress and Adventures. Uniform with "The Lilac Sunbonnet" and "Bog-Myrtle and Peat." Illustrated. 12mo. Cloth, $1.50.

It is safe to predict for the quaint and delightful figure of Cleg Kelly a notable place in the literature of the day. Mr. Crockett's signal success in his new field will enlarge the wide circle of his admirers. The lights and shadows of curious phases of Edinburgh life, and of Scotch farm and railroad life, are pictured with an intimate sympathy, richness of humor, and truthful pathos which make this new novel a genuine addition to literature. It seems safe to say that at least two characters—Cleg and Muckle Alick—are likely to lead Mr. Crockett's heroes in popular favor. The illustrations of this fascinating novel have been the result of most faithful and sympathetic study.

*B*OG-MYRTLE AND PEAT. Third edition. 12mo. Cloth, $1.50.

"Here are idyls, epics, dramas of human life, written in words that thrill and burn. . . . Each is a poem that has an immortal flavor. They are fragments of the author's early dreams, too bright, too gorgeous, too full of the blood of rubies and the life of diamonds to be caught and held palpitating in expression's grasp."—*Boston Courier.*

"Hardly a sketch among them all that will not afford pleasure to the reader for its genial humor, artistic local coloring, and admirable portrayal of character."—*Boston Home Journal.*

"One dips into the book anywhere and reads on and on, fascinated by the writer's charm of manner."—*Minneapolis Tribune.*

*T*HE LILAC SUNBONNET. Sixth edition. 12mo. Cloth, $1.50.

"A love story pure and simple, one of the old-fashioned, wholesome, sunshiny kind, with a pure-minded, sound-hearted hero, and a heroine who is merely a good and beautiful woman; and if any other love story half so sweet has been written this year, it has escaped our notice."—*New York Times.*

"The general conception of the story, the motive of which is the growth of love between the young chief and heroine, is delineated with a sweetness and a freshness, a naturalness and a certainty, which places 'The Lilac Sunbonnet' among the best stories of the time."—*New York Mail and Express.*

"In its own line this little love story can hardly be excelled. It is a pastoral, an idyl—the story of love and courtship and marriage of a fine young man and a lovely girl—no more. But it is told in so thoroughly delightful a manner, with such playful humor, such delicate fancy, such true and sympathetic feeling, that nothing more could be desired."—*Boston Traveller.*

THE ONE WHO LOOKED ON. By F. F. MON-
TRÉSOR, author of "Into the Highways and Hedges."
16mo. Cloth, special binding, $1.25.

"The story runs on as smoothly as a brook through lowlands; it ex-
cites your interest at the beginning and keeps it to the end."—*New York
Herald.*

"An exquisite story. . . . No person sensitive to the influence of what
makes for the true, the lovely, and the strong in human friendship and the
real in life's work can read this book without being benefited by it."—
Buffalo Commercial.

"The book has universal interest and very unusual merit. . . . Aside
from its subtle poetic charm, the book is a noble example of the power of
keen observation."—*Boston Herald.*

CORRUPTION. By PERCY WHITE, author of "Mr.
Bailey-Martin," etc. 12mo. Cloth, $1.25.

"There is intrigue enough in it for those who love a story of the ordinary kind, and the political part is perhaps more attractive in its sparkle
and variety of incident than the real thing itself."—*London Daily News.*

"A drama of biting intensity, a tragedy of inflexible purpose and relent-
less result."—*Pall Mall Gazette.*

A HARD WOMAN. A Story in Scenes. By VIOLET
HUNT. 12mo. Cloth, $1.25.

"An extremely clever work. Miss Hunt probably writes dialogue better than any of our young novelists. . . . Not only are her conversations
wonderfully vivacious and sustained, but she contrives to assign to each of
her characters a distinct mode of speech, so that the reader easily identifies
them, and can follow the conversations without the slightest difficulty."—
London Athenæum.

"One of the best writers of dialogue of our immediate day. The conversations in this book will enhance her already secure reputation."—*London Daily Chronicle.*

AN IMAGINATIVE MAN. By ROBERT S. HICH-
ENS, author of "The Green Carnation," etc. 12mo.
Cloth, $1.25.

"One of the brightest books of the year."—*Boston Budget.*

"Altogether delightful, fascinating, unusual."—*Cleveland Amusement
Gazette.*

"A study in character. . . . Just as entertaining as though it were the
conventional story of love and marriage. The clever hand of the author
of 'The Green Carnation' is easily detected in the caustic wit and pointed
epigram."—*Jeannette L. Gilder, in the New York World.*

TWO REMARKABLE AMERICAN NOVELS.

THE RED BADGE OF COURAGE. An Episode of the American Civil War. By STEPHEN CRANE. 12mo. Cloth, $1.00.

"Mr. Stephen Crane is a great artist, with something new to say, and consequently with a new way of saying it. . . . In 'The Red Badge of Courage' Mr. Crane has surely contrived a masterpiece. . . . He has painted a picture that challenges comparison with the most vivid scenes of Tolstoy's 'La Guerre et la Paix' or of Zola's 'La Débâcle.'"—*London New Review.*

"In its whole range of literature we can call to mind nothing so searching in its analysis, so manifestly impressed with the stamp of truth, as 'The Red Badge of Courage.' . . . A remarkable study of the average mind under stress of battle. . . . We repeat, a really fine achievement."—*London Daily Chronicle.*

'Not merely a remarkable book : it is a revelation. . . . One feels that, with perhaps one or two exceptions, all previous descriptions of modern warfare have been the merest abstractions."—*St. James Gazette.*

"Holds one irrevocably. There is no possibility of resistance when once you are in its grip, from the first of the march of the troops to the closing scenes. . . . Mr. Crane, we repeat, has written a remarkable book. His insight and his power of realization amount to genius."—*Pall Mall Gazette.*

IN DEFIANCE OF THE KING. A Romance of the American Revolution. By CHAUNCEY C. HOTCHKISS. 12mo. Paper, 50 cents ; cloth, $1.00.

"The whole story is so completely absorbing that you will sit far into the night to finish it. You lay it aside with the feeling that you have seen a gloriously true picture of the Revolution."—*Boston Herald.*

"The story is a strong one—a thrilling one. It causes the true American to flush with excitement, to devour chapter after chapter until the eyes smart; and it fairly smokes with patriotism."—*N. Y. Mail and Express.*

"The heart beats quickly, and we feel ourselves taking part in the scenes described. . . . Altogether the book is an addition to American literature."—*Chicago Evening Post.*

"One of the most readable novels of the year. . . . As a love romance it is charming, while it is filled with thrilling adventure and deeds of patriotic daring."—*Boston Advertiser.*

"This romance seems to come the nearest to a satisfactory treatment in fiction of the Revolutionary period that we have yet had."—*Buffalo Courier.*

"A clean, wholesome story, full of romance and interesting adventure. . . . Holds the interest alike by the thread of the story and by the incidents. . . . A remarkably well-balanced and absorbing novel."—*Milwaukee Journal.*

New York: D. APPLETON & CO., 72 Fifth Avenue.

*T*HE REDS OF THE MIDI. An Episode of the French Revolution. By FÉLIX GRAS. Translated from the Provençal by Mrs. CATHARINE A. JANVIER. With an Introduction by THOMAS A. JANVIER. With Frontispiece. 12mo. Cloth, $1.50.

M. Félix Gras is the official head of the *Félibrige*, the society of Provençal men of letters, the highest honor in their gift. It is believed that the introduction of his rare talent to our readers will meet with prompt appreciation.

"In all French history there is no more inspiring episode than that with which M. Gras deals in this story : the march to Paris and the doings in Paris of that Marseilles Battalion made up of men who were sworn to cast down 'the tyrant,' and who 'knew how to die.' His epitome of the motive power of the Revolution in the feelings of one of its individual peasant parts is the very essence of simplicity and directness. His method has the largeness and the clearness of the Greek drama. The motives are distinct. The action is free and bold. The climax is in evitable, and the story has a place entirely apart from all the fiction of the French Revolution with which I am acquainted."—*From Mr. Janvier's Introduction.*

*T*HE GODS, SOME MORTALS, AND LORD WICKENHAM. By JOHN OLIVER HOBBES. With Portrait. 12mo. Cloth, $1.50.

"Mrs. Craigie has taken her place among the novelists of the day. It is a high place and a place apart. Her method is her own, and she stands not exactly on the threshold of a great career, but already within the temple of fame."—*G. W. Smalley, in the Tribune.*

"Here is the sweetness of a live love story. . . . It is to be reckoned among the brilliants as a novel."—*Boston Courier.*

"One of the most refreshing novels of the period, full of grace, spirit, force, feeling, and literary charm."—*Chicago Evening Post.*

*M*AELCHO. By the Hon. EMILY LAWLESS, author of "Grania," "Hurrish," etc. 12mo. Cloth, $1.50.

"A paradox of literary genius. It is not a history, and yet has more of the stuff of history in it, more of the true national character and fate, than any historical monograph we know. It is not a novel, and yet fascinates us more than any novel."—*London Spectator.*

"Abounds in thrilling incidents. . . . Above and beyond all, the book charms by reason of the breadth of view, the magnanimity, and the tenderness which animate the author."—*London Athenæum.*

"A piece of work of the first order, which we do not hesitate to describe as one of the most remarkable literary achievements of this generation."—*Manchester Guardian.*

New York: D. APPLETON & CO., 72 Fifth Avenue.

"A better book than 'The Prisoner of Zenda.'"—*London Queen.*

*T*HE CHRONICLES OF COUNT ANTONIO. By
Anthony Hope, author of "The God in the Car," "The
Prisoner of Zenda," etc. With photogravure Frontispiece
by S. W. Van Schaick. Third edition. 12mo. Cloth,
$1.50.

"No adventures were ever better worth recounting than are those of
Antonio of Monte Velluto, a very Bayard among outlaws. . . . To all
those whose pulses still stir at the recital of deeds of high courage, we may
recommend this book. . . . The chronicle conveys the emotion of heroic
adventure, and is picturesquely written."—*London Daily News.*

"It has literary merits all its own, of a deliberate and rather deep
order. . . . In point of execution 'The Chronicles of Count Antonio' is
the best work that Mr. Hope has yet done. The design is clearer, the
workmanship more elaborate, the style more colored. . . . The incidents
are most ingenious, they are told quietly, but with great cunning, and the
Quixotic sentiment which pervades it all is exceedingly pleasant."—*Westminster Gazette.*

"A romance worthy of all the expectations raised by the brilliancy of
his former books, and likely to be read with a keen enjoyment and a
healthy exaltation of the spirits by every one who takes it up."—*The
Scotsman.*

"A gallant tale, written with unfailing freshness and spirit."—*London
Daily Telegraph.*

"One of the most fascinating romances written in English within many
days. The quaint simplicity of its style is delightful, and the adventures
recorded in these 'Chronicles of Count Antonio' are as stirring and ingenious as any conceived even by Weyman at his best."—*New York
World.*

"Romance of the real flavor, wholly and entirely romance, and narrated
in true romantic style. The characters, drawn with such masterly handling,
are not merely pictures and portraits, but statues that are alive and step
boldly forward from the canvas."—*Boston Courier.*

"Told in a wonderfully simple and direct style, and with the magic
touch of a man who has the genius of narrative, making the varied incidents
flow naturally and rapidly in a stream of sparkling discourse."—*Detroit
Tribune.*

"Easily ranks with, if not above, 'A Prisoner of Zenda.' . . . Wonderfully strong, graphic, and compels the interest of the most *blasé* novel
reader."—*Boston Advertiser.*

"No adventures were ever better worth telling than those of Count
Antonio. . . . The author knows full well how to make every pulse thrill,
and how to hold his readers under the spell of his magic."—*Boston Herald.*

"A book to make women weep proud tears, and the blood of men to
tingle with knightly fervor. . . . In 'Count Antonio' we think Mr. Hope
surpasses himself, as he has already surpassed all the other story-tellers of
the period."—*New York Spirit of the Times.*

A STREET IN SUBURBIA. By EDWIN PUGH. 12mo. Cloth, $1.00.

"Simplicity of style, strength, and delicacy of character study will mark this book as one of the most significant of the year."—*New York Press.*

"Thoroughly entertaining, and more—it shows traces of a creative genius something akin to Dickens."—*Boston Traveller.*

"In many respects the best of all the books of lighter literature brought out this season."—*Providence News.*

"A clever series of character sketches."—*Elmira Telegram.*

"Rippling over from end to end with fun and humor."—*London Academy.*

M AJESTY. A Novel. By LOUIS COUPERUS. Translated by A. TEIXEIRA DE MATTOS and ERNEST DOWSON. 12mo. Cloth, $1.00.

"No novelist whom we can call to mind has ever given the world such a masterpiece of royal portraiture as Louis Couperus's striking romance entitled 'Majesty.' "—*Philadelphia Record.*

"A very powerful and cleverly written romance."—*New York Times.*

"There is not an uninteresting page in the book, and it ought to be read by all who desire to keep in line with the best that is published in modern fiction."—*Buffalo Commercial.*

T HE NEW MOON. By C. E. RAIMOND, author of "George Mandeville's Husband," etc. 12mo. Cloth, $1.00.

"A delicate pathos makes itself felt as the narrative progresses, whose cadences fall on the spirit's consciousness with a sweet and soothing influence not to be measured in words."—*Boston Courier.*

"One of the most impressive of recent works of fiction, both for its matter and especially for its presentation."—*Milwaukee Journal.*

"The story is most graphically told, the characters are admirably drawn, and the moral of the whole thing is very desirable as inculcating an important lesson."—*Chicago Journal.*

"A surprisingly clever book in its way, being direct and simple, and true on every page to the author's purpose."—*New York Times.*

T HE WISH. A Novel. By HERMANN SUDERMANN. With a Biographical Introduction by ELIZABETH LEE. 12mo. Cloth, $1.00.

"Contains some superb specimens of original thought."—*New York World.*

"The style is direct and incisive, and holds the unflagging attention of the reader."—*Boston Journal.*

"A powerful story, very simple, very direct."—*Chicago Evening Post.*